Lady Harriet's Unusual Reward

Em Taylor

Copyright © 2015 Em Taylor

All rights reserved.

ISBN: 1515372448
ISBN-13: 978 - 1515372448

Edited by Em Petrova

DEDICATION

To my wee brother Colin who was the original inspiration for William but who actually is nothing like William except for having a kind heart and the ability to make me laugh.
To Tricia and Alison and everyone else at the castle. Thanks for the coffee and the company. You folks rock.
To Kirsty N who kept in touch
And to my family and friends in real life and online who cared during what has been a tough year.

Contents

Prologue	7
Chapter One	13
Chapter Two	18
Chapter Three	25
Chapter Four	33
Chapter Five	40
Chapter Six	47
Chapter Seven	55
Chapter Eight	59
Chapter Nine	70
Chapter Ten	79
Chapter Eleven	94
Chapter Twelve	101
Chapter Thirteen	115
Chapter Fourteen	138
Epilogue	153

Prologue

August 1821

Harriet scowled at the page she was reading. Really it was too much. This heroine was a complete ninny. Who would wander downstairs in just a nightrail in the middle of the night, calling out to alert a possible murderer that she was onto him? Not only that but why had she not taken a tinderbox to relight her candle when it had gone out? Or better still why not light the candles in the hallway? The foolish woman deserved to be murdered. Harriet just hoped the person downstairs was the devilishly handsome, but much misunderstood, Duke of Almondvale and not the murderous coalman. At least being forced to marry a duke would be better than the alternative.

A scream made Harriet jump and she lifted her head, blinking at the bright sunshine of the summer day. She'd heard a splash too—from the direction of the pond. If she recalled rightly, the pond in this area of the grounds was deep. If the person who had fallen in could not swim, they would likely be in trouble.

Harriet threw down the book, looking around but could see no one else. Not one other person from the large house party to celebrate Lady Hawthorne's sixtieth birthday party was anywhere in sight. That was a little odd. But it was rather warm and Harriet probably should not have been out in the midday sun herself.

She ran over to the pool and there, thrashing about in

the middle, was a little girl. She thought she may be Lord Stephen's daughter, but she could not be certain.

The child was quite a distance away. Too far to just lean out, grab her hand and pull her back to safety. Harriet kicked off her shoes, discarded her bonnet, and dived in. She began to kick her legs and push her arms through the water. It was difficult swimming in petticoats and a gown and they tangled around her legs, hampering her movements. Luckily the child was not far away and was managing to stay afloat. But the little creature was panicking and Harriet could see the fear in her big blue eyes.

After what seemed like an eternity Harriet was near enough to scoop the girl into her arms, flip onto her back and start swimming back towards the edge of the pool.

The girl was gasping, trying to speak. Harriet felt she should try to calm the child but she was struggling to breathe herself as she worked to get them back to safety. Every leg stroke was a kick to free her leg from her skirts as well as a kick against the water. The touch of the stone edge of the pond against the crown of her head told her they had made it. She dropped her legs and hoisted the child but it was no good. She was so tired.

"Hold on," she instructed. She gripped the pond's edge and tried to pull herself out. She seemed to weigh more than her horse. Possibly more than a coach and six. She dropped back into the water, defeated, and looked at the child. "What is your name?"

"Phoebe. Phoebe Charville."

"You're Lord Stephen Charville's daughter?" She had been correct.

"Y-yes." Her teeth were chattering.

"How old are you?"

"I'm four years o-old."

"Well that makes you a big girl and old enough to shout for help. You and I shall need to shout as loud as we can. So when I count to three we need to shout 'help.' Do you understand?"

Phoebe nodded.

"One, two, three."

****

Stephen had been searching for Phoebe for just a few minutes when an unholy racket started. It sounded like cats having their tails stood upon. Sounds that sent a knot of dread into his stomach. One of those cats was his daughter. He knew it and she was crying for his help.

God's teeth. She was in trouble.

He started running towards the sound heedless of any peril that may be ahead of him. Phoebe was in danger. He would not lose his baby. He'd already lost Sarah and he could not lose their daughter.

The noise was closer. He was drawing closer to the pond. A pair of women's slippers lay abandoned ahead of him in the grass. He stood on something. He glanced back to see what it was. A book.

When he got to the edge he looked down into the hole.

To the right side he saw two pairs of hands gripping the edge of the pond, and two wet, flushed faces still yelling for help. They had not noticed him.

"I'm here."

"Papa!"

Stephen moved along the pond and scooped his daughter out of the water. Then he reached down and pulled the young woman out too. She was heavy due to the amount of water her gown held. His gaze raked over the pair of them, assessing them for injuries. Phoebe seemed fine as she wrapped her arms around his waist and burrowed into him for warmth. The young woman seemed none the worse for wear either. Her lemon day dress hung off her, leaving little to the imagination. Only her stays preserved her modesty somewhat. He pulled off his coat and wrapped it around the woman and lifted Phoebe.

"Come let us get you back to the house. What happened?"

"I fell into the pond and this lady dived in, swam out and rescued me." Phoebe's teeth were chattering and she snuggled into his warmth. God help him, he'd nearly lost her.

"We need to get you both warmed up. I'll order hot baths and hot bricks for your beds. Maybe a tonic or something." The woman laughed as she wrung water from her copper hair. It looked dark now but he knew it would be much redder when dry. He now remembered who she was. Lady Harriet Weatherby. The daughter of the Earl of Oldbeck.

"I think Phoebe is more frightened than cold. It's a beautiful day. Plenty of people go swimming on such days. I'm sure as a boy you did. She will be fine. As will I. I am just a little shaken and tired as swimming in a gown is hard work."

"Her teeth are chattering, Lady Harriet and you are soaked through."

"And my hair will dry and my skin will dry and my clothes will be changed in a matter of minutes. Please do not worry on my account."

He nodded but steered her away from the main entrance to the manor. She gave him a curious glance.

"Your gown and petticoats are rather transparent, my lady. I think it best that you are seen by as few guests as possible." Gentlemanly honour dictated that he spare her the embarrassment of walking through a country manor in such a state but he also wanted to be the only man who had seen her like this. It was quite a delectable sight. And he felt like a cad that he was taking pleasure in the vision. But devil take it. He could not help that he was a man first and a gentleman second.

"Papa, Lady Harriet is correct. I am fine now."

"You are?"

"Yes."

"Well, let us see how you are once you are dried off in the nursery." The three made their way to Lady Harriet's room, then Phoebe and Stephen headed for the nursery where Stephen fussed and coddled until Nanny sent him away with warnings of dire consequences if he returned for the rest of the day.

Thus, Stephen was shocked when he arrived in the drawing room before dinner to find Lady Harriet already there, dressed in a light blue silk gown, looking well, a smile on her face, her dark auburn tresses piled high in an intricate coif and her cheeks a little too red from her time in the sun this afternoon.

He approached her and she turned a beatific smile on him. His insides did a rather pleasant little leap. Not since Sarah had been alive had a woman had this effect on him. His gaze dropped to her décolletage. Understated but enough of a hint of the pleasures that were to come should a man wish to sample. The very top of the line of her cleavage showed… just enough to tempt but not enough to make the ladies of the *ton* cast aspersions on her moral character. His blood heated at the thought of the temptations.

"Lady Harriet, I wanted to thank you for what you did today. You saved my daughter's life."

"I did nothing that anyone else who was there would not have done, my lord."

"That matters not. The fact is that you did it. You risked your own life to save Phoebe's and for that I am eternally grateful. I am forever in your debt. If there is anything—and I mean anything—I can do for you at any point in the future, you need only ask. If it is within my gift, it shall be yours. You have my word of honour as a gentleman. And remember, as the second son of a duke, there is not much that is not within my gift."

Harriet laughed at this. "You could always ask your big brother if you can't help."

He chuckled.

"Oh, I never ask Theodore for anything."

"I shall bear that in mind.

"Please do. But remember. Whatever you need is yours. You only have to ask."

With that he bowed and took his place in line for dinner as the gong sounded.

Chapter One

August 1823

"Have you seen Lord Oldbeck, Mrs Aitken?" Harriet asked as she avoided the man dismantling the fortune teller's booth.

"Not for some time, my lady."

"Oh dear, I hope he's not up to mischief. That brother of mine is always up to something. I really do despair of him at times."

"I saw him with Mary Callahan the kitchen maid, maybe about three quarters of an hour ago," said Tommy Galloway as he walked by carrying a couple of large planks of wood. "They was heading t'wards the stables."

Harriet and Mrs Aitken exchanged a glance then started walking in the direction of the stables.

"You don't think they're getting up to no good, do you, my lady?"

"Oh I wouldn't think so. No." Harriet shook her head vociferously. There was no way. William wouldn't ruin the girl. He was simple-minded of course. And so was Mary, the kitchen maid. But he knew the basics. Didn't he? And Mary's mother would have explained things. Surely to God, she would have prepared the girl for the world. Or would she? Mary had been young when Mrs Callahan had passed on. At what age did most young girls of that station learn such things? Perhaps Mary was too young to learn about men and their desires when her parents had died.

Once they reached the stables they found the stable master leading a beautiful brown gelding out.

"Your brother is in the barn, my lady. He's with the kitchen maid, Mary. You know. The one that's well... you know. Not very clever, like."

"I see."

"They was quite umm, amorous."

"Thank you."

The two women hurried over the cobbled yard without saying anything.

Kissing. She prayed to God he only meant kissing. The barn door was shut but she could hear her brother's voice around the corner. He had used the small side door for his assignation.

"I love you, Mary. But I think Harry will be mad."

"Mrs Aitken will be mad too, and cook."

"We'll keep it our secret. Did I hurt you really badly?"

"No. Only at first it hurt. But then it got better. And then..."

There were a couple of soft thuds on the wood and muffled grunts and a moan.

Mrs Aitken coughed loudly and Mary yelped.

The two women walked sedately around the corner. Harriet wanted to die.

Her brother's shirt was undone, his cravat was gone. Heaven alone knew where it was. His shirt sleeves were rolled up and his shirt tails hung out of his breeches. She noted with dismay that his breeches' buttons were done up in the wrong order too.

The maid's hair was unbound. Chestnut hair flowed down to her waist. Her ruddy cheeks flamed, partly with passion, partly with embarrassment. Her dress was torn slightly at the breast and there was a dark wet patch at the back just at the top of her thighs.

"Well, my lady, either her courses have come early or your brother has breached her maidenhead," whispered the housekeeper to Harriet. The look in the woman's eyes held no reproach, just concern for the mess they might all have just found themselves in.

"It's not Mary's fault," shouted William, pulling his beloved into his arms and shielding her from the wrath he expected from his sister. Harriet could feel the tears nip at the back of her eyes and threaten to spill. If only Papa was still here. He'd know what to do.

Harriet held out a calming hand to her brother.

"William, neither you nor Mary are in trouble. But we need to get Mary inside and bathed."

"I love her," he said sullenly.

"I know." Harriet smiled encouragingly at him. Her little brother stood six foot tall and about three foot wide holding the petite maid against him like a precious doll. He had the thinking capacity of a six-year-old but an ability to love of twenty men. "Here is what is going to happen. You are going to the stable to ask for a blanket. Mary needs a blanket to get back to the house. Her dress has blood on it. You don't want everyone to know what you two have been up to. Not everyone will approve and you need to look after Mary's reputation."

"I don't want Mary's reputation harmed," William replied hastily.

"Of course you do not. So leave Mary with us and go and get the blanket. She's not in any trouble. Then Mrs Aitken will take her back to the servants' quarters and get her cleaned up. Is that all right?"

He nodded, passed his beloved Mary over to his sister and headed off to the stables.

"Are you all right, Mary?" Mrs Aitken asked.

"Oh yes. William is lovely. I love him too."

"You do. And when William, umm, when he, when his seed came out of him... was he inside you, my love?"

"Oh yes. It was lovely and warm. He said it was the best moment of his life."

"Right."

Harriet's cheeks were burning but she was grateful to the housekeeper for establishing the facts such as they were. And she was grateful she at least had a rudimentary understanding of animal husbandry that she knew what the woman was asking.

"It is dripping down my leg now though. I do really need that bath." She swiped between her legs with her skirts, her lips curled slightly.

"Ah here's the earl. Thank heavens," Harriet said. This had to be the worst day of her life.

Mary was bustled off by Mrs Aitken, and William threw his arm around his big sister.

"Harry, you are the best big sister ever. And today was great. The summer fete was the best ever. Did you see the fortune teller? She said I was going to marry and have three children. I think she knew about Mary. And I won the sack race."

"Did you?"

"You are mad about Mary, are you not?"

"No, William. It's just that what you did with Mary might have consequences. You know that what you did might result in her having a baby, do you not?"

"I suppose but I didn't think. We were kissing and it was lovely then *that* grew hard and it felt so right and Harry, have you ever done it?"

"William, we are not discussing me."

"Oh. Well it feels so good. And if you had done it you would know and you wouldn't scold me. Though it must be different for girls because you do not have a rod."

"A rod?"

"Mmm, that's what the stable hands call it."

"It is?" Now she understood why some families just sent people like William off to institutions and washed their hands of them. She loved her brother completely but he was such hard work at times and now she had no close relatives left, she had no one left to lean on.

"Yes, and when I put it into Mary it was…"

"ENOUGH!"

"What? See, I knew you were mad."

"I am not mad, William but it is not polite to discuss… bed sport in public and it is certainly not the done thing to discuss it with one's siblings."

"Oh I see."

"I hope so. And I also hope Mary is not increasing because if she is, well, I'm damned if I know how we're going to get out of that mess without a huge scandal on our heads."

If truth be told, an earl leaving a simple kitchen maid with his bastard child in her belly was hardly scandalous. It happened the length and breadth of Britain on a monthly basis Harriet would wager. But the earl in question was an imbecile and in love with the aforementioned maid. Harriet's conscience would not allow her to pay Mary off—not for Mary's sake nor for William's sake. And not only that, but Harriet was beginning to suspect that she could not handle William or the estate on her own. She was going to need reinforcements and the reinforcements would have to be male. It looked as if she was going to have to marry.

Chapter Two

Six weeks later

Harriet looked up from the ledger she was poring over and smiled at Mrs Aitken and the footman. Joe laid the tea tray on the desk, bowed and exited.

"Thank you," she said to the back of the servant and to Mrs Aitken. "I need a rest. I cannot look at this any longer. I do not understand it at all. Mr Holroyd wants me to make a decision about planting next year but I honestly have no idea what to say to him. My governesses taught me how to embroider samplers and play the pianoforte. They never covered crop rotation and animal husbandry. And I have tried to read some of these books, but I think Papa's books may be somewhat out of date for modern farming methods."

"The earl has been in the kitchen again and has taken Mary away from her duties, Lady Harriet."

Harriet ground her teeth. How many times had they had this discussion? How many times had she told William he could not just take the maid away from her job?

"Has he?"

"Yes. And my lady, you know it has been six weeks since we found his lordship and Mary outside the barn after their first time and Mary has not been to me for anything for her courses. The maids always come to me."

"You think she is with child."

"I believe she may be."

"I see."

"My lady, they have been, umm, together since then. Her dresses have been stained a few times and your brother's sheets show evidence of him taking her to his bedchamber."

Something caught Harriet's attention out of the side window of the study. She turned her head to see William kissing Mary outside—for all the world to see. His hand cupped her breast and played with it in a most scandalous fashion.

"Oh God." She stood and ran out the door, through the foyer and down the steps of the house. She didn't care that she was no longer being ladylike. As she approached her brother she was gasping for air.

He looked up and rolled his eyes. "Harry, go away."

"No," she hissed. "I will not go away. You are behaving in a most ungentlemanly manner and you are going to cause terrible scandal for Mary." He had the decency to look a little chagrined. "You cannot grope a lady in public like that, William. It is unseemly."

"They are a little sore, William," whispered Mary.

"Oh I am sorry. I did not mean to hurt you, Mary. I would never hurt you."

"I know, my love."

He smiled at the endearment.

"And you cannot keep taking Mary away from her duties."

"I can if I want to. I am the earl."

"That is precisely why you cannot. You have responsibilities. To your station and to your staff. If you take Mary away, other staff have to do her work."

"Stop trying to be in charge, Harry. You are not in charge."

"I am in charge. Papa put me in charge."

"No, he did not. I'm the earl and you're just a girl."

"But I am the eldest."

God, she felt like she was eight years old again.

"I'm taking Mary to my bedchamber and you can't stop me, and I'm going to tup her."

He took the maid's hand and marched her off in the direction of the house. Mrs Aitken was at her side. She had heard most of the conversation.

"What are you going to do now, my lady?"

"Firstly I am going to find whichever stable hand taught William the word 'tup' and strangle him, and then I'm going to load William, Mary, you and me in a carriage and go to London. A couple of years ago a gentleman promised me that if I ever needed anything—anything at all and it was within his gift to give it to me, he would. Time to see exactly how far gentlemanly honour really does stretch. Will it stretch as far as the altar, do you think, Mrs Aitken?"

****

"Papa!"

Lord Stephen Charville, brother of the Duke of Halimead and next in line to the title should some hideous accident befall his brother Theodore, looked up from the missive he was writing to the dowager duchess, as a six-year-old bundle of pink muslin, ribbons and brown ringlets came rushing into his study and threw herself at him. He turned his chair and lifted Phoebe onto his lap, hugging her as he looked up into the stern eyes of his sister-in-law.

He raised an eyebrow, daring her to say anything.

Yes, he spoiled his precocious daughter. And how dare she chastise him for it with her haughty aristocratic sniff.

"How was Hyde Park? Did you see the ducks?"

"Yes, and a few swans."

"And were you good for your Aunt Elizabeth?"

"Mostly."

"Mostly? That is not good enough, Miss Charville. You

must always follow Aunt Elizabeth's instructions. You know this and we have talked about it. We shall discuss it later." He pushed a large finger through one of her brown ringlets. Her hair was so like her mother's and it made him smile in remembrance of Sarah's trilling laughter and devil-may-care attitude to life. But he wasn't melancholy as many seemed to think he was. He wasn't anything really. He didn't care enough even to be sad.

Except about Phoebe. He cared about Phoebe.

"I am sorry, Papa. I will listen to Aunt Elizabeth's instructions in future. Clara and I knew we were not supposed to run but we were just so excited when we saw the family of squirrels."

"I see. Well, your aunt has that look on her face that says she wants to scold me so take Clara up to the nursery. I'm sure Nanny can find you some milk and biscuits and keep you amused for now while I take my lecture."

Elizabeth harrumphed but did not deny it, coming further into the room to allow Phoebe's escape. It was amazing that two six-year-old girls could sound so much like a herd of elephants running up one staircase.

He motioned to the two high-backed chairs at the hearth, pulled the bell cord and ordered tea when the butler appeared. He looked his sister-in-law up and down as if considering a horse for sale at Tattersall's.

He understood why Theo had married her. She was the daughter of an earl, demure, pretty, buxom, wide-hipped, accomplished and clever. Her taste in clothes for the most part was exemplary except…

"Lizzie, what the hell are you wearing on your head? It looks as if a bird's nest fell on you while you were in Hyde Park."

Elizabeth sniffed disdainfully at her brother-in-law and adjusted the monstrosity.

"I assure you, my lord, it is the height of fashion. Not that you would know, cooped up in here, day after day. When was the last time you went riding during the fashionable hour, or attended a ball or a rout or even went to your club?"

"It seems as if it's rather dangerous to go out in London these days if random bird's nests are going to fall on my head," he said, grinning. "I'm surprised half the pigeons in London did not attack, trying to mate with that bonnet. That would have been a sight to see. Almost worth going out for."

"Stephen, you are beastly."

"Yes, I am rather. That is why it is best that I stay in. It means I am only beastly to those forced into my company by dint of birth or marriage."

A footman arrived with a tea tray and the conversation halted for a few moments. As soon as the servant left, Elizabeth poured the tea then began her attack.

"I am concerned about Phoebe."

"Oh God, here we go. Lizzie, I haven't sold her to the local chimney sweep. She is fine."

"Stop blaspheming and she is not fine. She does not have to be a street urchin to be harmed by your neglect."

Stephen laid his cup on the side table, afraid he would either break it in his hands or throw it into the fireplace… or worse… at Elizabeth.

"I do not neglect my daughter, Elizabeth."

"Stephen, her dresses are getting too small. She needs a governess, not a nanny. She's wild and uncontrolled. She needs to learn to be a lady. She should be learning embroidery and to play the pianoforte."

"There is time for that. And you always deal with her clothes anyway. So do whatever it is you do and send me the bill."

"We are going back to the country tomorrow, Stephen. Theodore does not want me to be rushing around so. He wants me to rest this time."

"This time?"

"Yes. This time. I am increasing again. Third time lucky since Clara hopefully."

"Oh Lizzie. Congratulations."

She held out her hand.

"No, not yet. It is too soon."

He nodded.

"I understand. I hope it goes well for you."

"You need to change your lifestyle, Stephen. For the sake of Phoebe. For the sake of yourself. Perhaps you could remarry."

"No." He did not even need to consider the possibility. He did not want to remarry.

"Sarah would not have wanted this."

"It has nothing to do with Sarah. It is what I want."

"No one believes that, Stephen—least of all you." With that, the Duchess of Halimead stood, brushed down her skirts and swept out of the room. He heard her ask the footman to arrange for her daughter to be fetched and a few minutes later his relatives taking their leave.

She was wrong, of course. He missed Sarah. He had loved the woman with all his heart. But he was not one of those tragic heroes, lost forever and unable to bear the idea of another in his wife's bed. But as with everything else in life, since Sarah he was just not interested. Life held no spark. As a second son he had no estate to run, no fortune to invest. Oh yes, he had money and enough of it to live out his days and for his daughter to have a substantial dowry. Had he chosen to marry again and had a son and more children, they would have wanted for nothing. He was very well heeled.

Life was just rather grey. The only colour in it was Phoebe, and a six-year-old could not hold his attention for too long. She was in bed early in the evening, in the nursery for most of the day. And frankly, the lives of the idle rich annoyed him. Nothing irritated him more than gossiping women and nattering gentlemen. Oftentimes the male of the species were worse than the females.

Marriage would be a disaster. A woman would nag and hound him. He'd be dragged to balls and other *ton* entertainments.

He would need to find out about getting a governess for Phoebe. He moved back to his desk and to the missive he had just started writing to his mama. She would know who to ask. And then he needed to work out how to get the child some new clothes. Lizzie had always seen to her clothes. Would a governess deal with such things? What about his housekeeper?

Devil take it. He couldn't take her into a ladies dressmaker. And is that where little girls were fitted for dresses anyway? He would ask his mother that too.

He dipped his quill into the ink.

Damn, sometimes Lizzie did make a good point.

Chapter Three

Harriet moved Mary's arm out of the way and tugged on the muslin of her gown. It made a satisfying ripping sound and Harriet looked down at the frayed edged just at Mary's waist.

"My lady, you ripped my dress."

Harriet tried to look apologetic but she suspected that she failed miserably as she turned her face towards the maid-turned-companion.

"I know, I am sorry but it was necessary."

"Necessary for what?"

"I need time alone with Lord Stephen so I need a reason for you to leave the room. You will be taken away to have your gown mended."

"Oh." Harriet could tell that Mary was still rather confused. They were sitting in the drawing room of Lord Stephen Charville's townhouse in South Audley Street awaiting his return.

The entire trip to London had been fraught, with William being truculent and ornery, claiming he wanted to stay in the country with his horse. He hated London and all its restrictions and Harriet understood. People stared at him and his odd behaviour. Ladies tittered behind their fans. And she regularly felt traitorous towards her brother for feeling embarrassed by him. He could not help that he spoke too loudly or out of turn at times. He laughed in the wrong place when they went to the theatre or rushed up to pet horses at the side of the road. Sometimes he would give coins to street urchins for no apparent reason.

On their one night in a coaching inn, Harriet had been forced to share a room with Mary to stop William from bedding the girl. And she knew they had spent the night together last night in the town house. The whole situation was untenable. They were going to have to marry—and soon.

There was one positive thing. Mary could at least speak with proper diction. It turned out that Mary's mother had been a lady's maid and had taught her daughter to speak properly. It was not until the girl was about six that it became clear that Mary lacked the mental capacity of other girls. Unable to grasp the basics of letters and numbers, her mother had taught her basic housekeeping skills. When Olive Callahan died, Mary was twelve years old and the girl was already working in the kitchens of Oldbeck House. Her father had died when she was a baby—from a mining accident.

For now Harriet had decided to pass Mary off as her companion as she went about town. Mary was wearing one of her old gowns. Mrs Aitken had hurriedly hemmed it as the former maid was a couple of inches shorter than Harriet, but the fit was reasonable.

The front door opened and closed and Harriet heard a quiet discussion in the hallway. She was sure that Lord Stephen would be surprised at her visit and even more surprised that when she had found him not at home she had insisted on waiting. It was not the done thing but desperate times called for desperate measures.

Lord Stephen walked into the drawing room and Harriet and Mary stood to greet him. Harriet noticed out of the corner of her eye that Mary's attention was on the rip on her dress and not their host. She moved her hand slightly to tap the girl and draw her attention back to his lordship. Thankfully it worked and Mary dutifully curtseyed when Harriet did. Lord Stephen bowed and gestured for them to take a seat.

"Oh, I wondered if perhaps someone would be able to help out my companion, Miss Callahan. Her gown was caught on a railing and was ripped as we walked down Curzon Street. She is rather distressed about it. Perhaps one of your maids is handy with a needle and thread."

"Oh of course. Though it would leave you unchaperoned, Lady Harriet. I would not want…"

"I am sure your staff can be trusted, my lord. Your butler appears to be a man of the utmost discretion." Harriet turned her gaze on the man still standing in the doorway. He drew himself up to his full height.

"Of course, my lady."

"And you are a gentleman, are you not, Lord Stephen? Surely I am safe with you."

"Well of course, Lady Harriet."

"Then that is settled. Miss Callahan?" She gestured to the door and Mary did as she was bid, curtseying to Lord Stephen and her mistress as she left.

Harriet turned to her prey and smiled.

"Please take a seat, Lady Harriet. I must say, you have me intrigued."

Harriet sat on the chaise she and Mary had been occupying until recently. Her façade was dropping now that he was here. Bravado was all well and good but it took real courage to carry out her plan.

"I do apologise for just appearing without an invitation, my lord."

She looked up into kind brown eyes. He waved away the apology as if social mores were of no consequence.

"Please, my lady, do not think on it."

"You did say that day, when your daughter fell in the pond, that if I ever needed anything—anything at all—I must come to you."

He nodded gravely.

"I did."

She swallowed hard.

"I need a husband."

****

If Lady Harriet Weatherby had stood up and kicked him in the balls, Stephen could not have been more stunned. *A husband.* He blinked. Then he blinked again as his gaze swept up the young woman seated in front of him, all blue muslin and femininity, biting her lip suggestively in a most innocent fashion. Her eyelids fluttered as if she had shocked herself with the brazenness of her own suggestion.

Her fingers tangled in the tie of her reticule and she lowered her gaze.

"It is not for me. It is for my brother, you see."

"For your brother?" he choked. "Lady Harriet, I am pretty sure that the Archbishop of Canterbury will not provide a special licence for me to marry your brother. He may be a doddering old fool but even he is not that senile."

"No!" The frustration was evident in her voice. "You would marry me. But I need to marry for my brother's sake."

"You do? Who on earth is your brother?"

"The Earl of Oldbeck."

Stephen wracked his brains. He never paid much attention to Debrett's. His mother and Elizabeth would have known who the hell the Earl of Oldbeck was but he was all at sea on this one. Certainly not someone with whom he had attended Eton. Did she need money? No, that could not be it. She would be the one bringing the dowry. Was she with child? But then why would that affect her brother? Brothers were never troubled by the scandals of their sisters. He narrowed his gaze on her and a flicker of memory came to him. "Ah your brother is William. He is the imbecile, is he not?"

"Yes." Her voice was quiet.

"You do not like that word, do you?"

"I prefer not to use it, my lord."

"Then I apologise for using it."

"William cannot count and has difficulty reading. His manners are not always what they should be. He can be loud and brash and is often childish in his understanding of the world. But he is not always as daft as people make him out to be." Her words were defensive and there was fire in her green eyes. Her chin was raised as she made her little speech. "But he cannot run an estate. He has discovered the fairer sex—Miss Callahan in particular. He says they are in love. She says they are in love too. He will not follow my instructions. He is a child trapped in a man's body with a man's… urges and I cannot cope." Tears welled in her eyes now as her arms waved in front of her.

The poor girl was nearly having a fit of the vapours and his heart went out to her. He wondered what it would be like trying to deal with Phoebe with her childish wishes to climb trees and feed the ducks but grown up with a woman's urges to flirt with men and bring them home to her bed. The thought did not bear thinking about. He'd lock her in her bloody room.

"Can you not send Miss Callahan away? Is she just your companion?"

"She was the kitchen maid until a few days ago and now she is increasing."

"A kitchen maid? Give her a cottage in the village and a stipend and send her on her way."

Lady Harriet's mouth fell open, her eyes wide.

"You are a brute. Why do men seem to think that everything can be fixed with a dank little cottage and a yearly sum of money? The girl is just like William. She is not able to fend for herself. William loves her. Love is all he has to give."

"He has money."

"Spoken like a true aristocrat," she observed tartly.

Stephen sat back on his seat and studied the young woman in the blue day gown as she removed a handkerchief from her reticule and dabbed her eyes and nose. Once she had composed herself she turned to him.

"So, my lord, do I take it that you are no longer an honourable gentleman and I am to leave here without my reward for saving your daughter's life?"

"Would you let me try to help your brother without marrying you? You need help. I understand that. Perhaps I could honour my vow to you by giving you help with the earl. A guiding hand, as it were. Then if it does not work, I shall indeed marry you as you have asked."

"I… I suppose that might work," Lady Harriet answered, looking somewhat sceptical. "You have a week."

"Come now, Lady Harriet. You do not want to marry a dried up old cynic like me."

"I must admit, I have not thought too hard about actually being married to you, my lord. My concern is for William."

He allowed his gaze to rake over her. Best that she realise this was not a game. If he was to end up marrying her, it would be a proper marriage. He may not have much of a notion for the fairer sex these days but he did remember his reaction to this pretty little thing in her wet transparent gown. She had haunted his dreams for weeks after that house party. And truthfully, in the six years since Sarah's death, she had been the only woman who had stirred him beyond a single fantasy.

He may as well put the prim and proper miss off the idea completely. He was not going to allow her to upset his perfectly easy, grey and unexceptional life with her burnished red hair, her emerald eyes sparkling defiantly at him and her pink cheeks burning red with embarrassment or anger, he wasn't sure. He allowed his gaze to linger on her décolletage for a moment.

"Well, that is probably for the best, my lady, as I would be pretty insatiable. It has been rather a long time since a pretty lady has warmed my bed sheets."

She heaved in a breath, improving her décolletage and stirring parts of his anatomy he had to will not to be stirred.

"My lord, that is not proper."

"That is precisely why you want me to succeed with my plan and not have to move on to yours, my lady."

He gave her a wicked grin as Miss Callahan hurried back into the room.

"I do apologise my lady. I cast up my accounts just as they were finishing. Luckily I made it to the necessary in time. Everyone says this is going to keep happening for another couple of months."

Tears welled in the girl's eyes.

"Ginger," said Stephen quickly. "Suck on ginger and that should help. My wife had to do that for the first three months she was increasing. Helped immeasurably."

"Oh!" Miss Callahan said. "Thank you, my lord." Then she turned to Lady Harriet. "I thought you said it was a secret."

"It is, but Lord Stephen is different. He is going to help us."

"Yes, Lord Oldbeck and I are old friends. In fact I am returning with you to your townhouse to see him. I shall just arrange for our outdoor clothing."

"Oh, he will be pleased to see you," Mary said, hurrying for the door.

"She gets a little excited," Lady Harriet said, apologetically.

He smiled reassuringly.

"Please do not concern yourself, Lady Harriet. I understand the situation and do not judge Miss Callahan. Nor will I judge your brother." He watched her features relax somewhat. This was going to be an interesting week, he suspected. The grey in his life seemed to be dissipating and blue and lemon were beginning to take its place.

Of course dealing with Harriet's brother was going to

be no mean feat. Not because of the brother, but because of the lady herself. She obviously liked to be in control and making her relinquish it was going to take cunning and guile. But devil take it. He loved a woman with spirit, who was bossy and who had such an attractive flush to her cheek and to the slender columns of her neck. And as for that bosom…

Oh God, he was done for.

Chapter Four

They arrived in the townhouse on Curzon Street after much fuss. Lord Stephen had insisted on bringing around his carriage pointing out that being seen with him walking all the way along South Audley Street, then all the way along Curzon Street would cause no end of gossip, especially if Miss Callahan's gown was prone to meet with accidents. He had said this in a way that suggested he was suspicious of the first accident. And Harriet could not really blame him.

"Mary, go to your room and change into your pink gown. We should get that gown mended properly. Tomorrow we shall go shopping and get you some new clothes—ones more befitting a ladies companion."

"Yes, my lady."

She curtseyed and scurried off.

"Harry, is that you?" William's voice was loud and clear as he yelled from the study into the foyer. She rolled her eyes.

"I shall be with you presently, William," she called delicately, enough to be heard but not loud enough to sound brash.

She shed her pelisse, bonnet and gloves and handed them to the butler along with her reticule. Her companion handed the servant his hat and gloves. She gestured in the direction of the study.

"Aye, Harry, this book talks about building a treehouse.

We should do that. Then you cannot complain about me taking Mary to the barn to tup her."

"William!"

They walked into the study to find William, his booted feet up on the desk and his nose in a book called "Great Wheezes for Young Gentlemen."

"What? Honestly, Harriet, this says it is really easy and there is plenty of wood around the estate. Let us go home to Oldbeck and forget whatever nonsense you have planned for us here. You know I hate London." His sentence ended on a childish whine.

"We are home and I have told you before not to use that word. It is impolite and not to be used, especially when we have a visitor." Her last words came out on a hiss and William at last looked past her to Lord Stephen.

"Well how was I to know we had a visitor?"

"You should not be shouting that word around the house, William." Honestly, her patience was as thin as lace at present.

She felt a hand on her elbow for just a second. It was reassuring and then it was gone as Lord Stephen walked farther into the room.

"Oldbeck, pleasure to meet you, old chap. It has been a long time. So sorry to hear about your father."

"Ah yes." William suddenly remembered himself and shuffled to his feet, bowing. "I am sorry, I…"

"Lord Stephen Charville, brother to the Duke of Halimead. It is all right. No one expects you to remember everyone. I appreciate you have been in mourning for your father and therefore out of society. My deepest condolences for your loss, my lord."

"Thank you." Stephen looked at Harriet and she gave him an encouraging smile. It was not often that anyone spoke to William as if he was a member of the peerage.

"So you have a young lady I hear."

"Yes. Mary. She is beautiful and I love her."

"I see. And while I do understand how you feel about

her, I'm afraid the ladies just do not like such vulgar language in their presence. Genteel ladies like your sister and your lovely Mary should not have to hear words that the stable lads use. Ladies like to be wooed with the words of the poets. So my advice is keep the bawdy language for when you are among men, and even then, keep it to a minimum. Now, where's the brandy?"

"Brandy?" Harriet had been impressed until that moment and the word came out like a washer-woman's screech. "William does not drink brandy, your lordship. Please, do not lead him into bad habits and debauchery."

Lord Stephen chuckled and looked at William.

"I am sorry, Oldbeck, do you mind if I step out and have a quick word with Lady Harriet? I shall make sure the butler returns with some brandy. Then perhaps we can go to White's. Are you a member of any of the gentlemen's clubs in town?"

"No."

"Was your father?"

"He was a member of White's."

"Oh well, it is a family tradition. We would not want to break it, would we? Thank God. I am not sure I fancy Boodle's or Brooks'."

William laughed at that and Lord Stephen moved to leave the room. Harriet preceded him out, hurrying into the drawing room opposite. He seemed upset with her but it was she who should be upset with him. Introducing William to spirits was the last thing he should be doing. Look what havoc had been wreaked when he had discovered the fairer sex. God help her if William started getting foxed. There would be more than one maid in the town carrying his progeny.

"Harriet, it really is not proper for you to tell a peer of the realm what he can and cannot drink once he has reached his majority, now is it?"

"I... I beg your pardon!" She knew her mouth was gaping and she could not form a coherent sentence in her head. How dare Lord Stephen speak to her in such a manner? "My Lord, I beseech you…"

Lord Stephen's chuckle was low and his eyes glinted with merriment.

"Tell me, my lady, how did you feel just then when I withdrew your title and scolded you?"

"I… My lord that was quite undignified."

"Did you feel… oh I don't know… like a little girl, still in the schoolroom being scolded?"

"A little."

"Did you feel as if your place in society was worthless?"

"To an extent."

"How many people call your brother Oldbeck?"

Harriet thought for a moment.

"None that I can think of."

"Do you know how many people call me Stephen?"

"No."

"My mother. And occasionally my sister-in-law when she is not completely vexed with me. For the most part I am Charville and my brother is Halimead. Only his wife, my mother and occasionally I call him Theo and even then only in private. Yet you think it is acceptable to call your brother William, even in front of a man who has a mere honorary title."

"What are you trying to say, my lord?"

"I am trying to say that if you continue to treat your brother like a child, he will continue to act like a child, my lady."

"But he thinks like a child," she said, her tone urgent. Did he not understand?

"Perhaps. But he does understand that he should not speak in such a manner when ladies are around. He just wants to shock and vex you. You are correct. He does need a man around to look up to and to try to emulate. But, Lady Harriet, gentlemen drink brandy and spend time in gentlemen's clubs. If I am going to teach Lord Oldbeck to be a gentleman, I shall do it correctly."

"So you will marry me?"

He laughed and tipped her chin with his knuckle—a gesture that seemed rather familiar considering they hardly knew each other.

"Not so fast, my lady. You make a very tempting offer but I like my life as it is. I have my daughter and my space and no one to bother me. I do need a little information from you though. Where does one get gowns for a six-year-old girl and where does one find a governess?"

"Is this for Phoebe?"

"No, I was thinking of taking up the pianoforte and had decided that breeches and waistcoats were not my style after all."

Harriet cocked her head to one side and considered him and his dry wit.

"I hear they require new players at Drury Lane, my lord. I am also informed that it is common for second sons to be bored and to consider a life on the stage. I think you would be well-suited."

His mouth twitched and she knew she had matched him adequately.

"Clever and beautiful," he murmured.

"I shall have the answer to both questions by the time you come back. I asked Mr Holroyd, our man of business, to find a governess who was willing to take on a… umm… well a charge who would be a little different… I mean Mary, and to school her in the ways of being a lady. Perhaps we could work together on this?"

"You mean my daughter and your maid?" His eyes opened wide and he looked aghast.

"I mean my companion and soon-to-be sister-in-law and your six-year-old daughter. Yes."

"Is she likely to talk about tupping in front of my daughter?"

"Oh no. Mary is very polite. She gets very upset when William mentions it."

"I see." A smile spread across his lips. "Mary may get upset but Lady Harriet blushes whenever anyone says tupping."

"You just told my brother that it is not the done thing to mention it in front of his sister."

"I did, did I not? Shame really, because you become even more pretty when you blush."

"My Lord, this is not appropriate."

"I thought you wanted to marry me."

"I do, but…" There was not really anything she could say to that. She had painted herself into this corner.

"Find a governess for Mary and Phoebe. It will do neither of them any harm to spend time with someone from out with their own social class. Do not meddle in how I handle your brother. He needs to become a man and a gentleman. He needs to know when to stand up for himself, when to back down, when to stand his ground, when to walk away and when it is appropriate to let a lady know he appreciates her."

He tilted her chin again and captured her green gaze with his dark brown one. She was only vaguely aware of his warm hand wrapping around her fingers and lifting it to his lips, pressing it ever so softly to the warm mouth, holding it there for a scandalously long time, allowing his breath to caress her knuckles, Then he stepped back, let go of her hand and bowed courteously and respectfully as if nothing untoward had just taken place.

Her mind was like mashed potato and something was happening in the secret place between her legs which did not bear thinking about. She was hot and cold all at the same time. And he was gone, checking with the butler that he had delivered the brandy. Good grief! Was this a fit of the vapours she was having? She had never had one before, but she was all of a flutter.

Tea. She needed tea. It was the only cure. Mama had said it cured everything. Oh dear. What had she done—inviting this scoundrel into their lives? *Nothing good comes of second sons*. That's what Great Aunt Agatha had always said. Perhaps she had been right. The man was a menace.

Oh, where was that tea? Oh, she had not rung for it. Oh, he had got her all hot and bothered. It was for the best he had refused her offer of marriage. It was becoming clear now.

Chapter Five

"Whittingham, may I introduce Oldbeck. Oldbeck, this is Whittingham. We shared a room at Eton together."

"And a few other things if memory serves correctly," drawled his friend, nodding at Oldbeck in a friendly manner, before raising an eyebrow so slightly at Stephen that only a close observer would notice. A miniscule shake of the head on Stephen's part was met with a smile for their new friend. "Terribly sorry to hear about your father, Oldbeck. Will you be taking up his seat in the House?"

"I do not know. I was invited but we have not been to London since he died and…"

The poor fellow was getting flustered and looked to Stephen for help. Stephen gave him a reassuring grin and placed a hand on his shoulder.

"Time enough for that yet, Oldbeck. Parliament is barely finished for the Season. We can discuss it some other time. What are you drinking, Whittingham?"

"Claret."

The man called over a footman and ordered drinks for the two newcomers and Stephen indicated a seat for William and took another. William fidgeted and for the first time Stephen wondered if this had been a good idea.

"The weather," Oldbeck said suddenly. Whittingham and Stephen both turned questioning looks on him. "Mama used to say when in company one should talk about the weather. And Harriet says not to mention tupping." Whittingham roared with laughter, drawing a few gazes of older gentleman as Stephen slapped Oldbeck on the back and chuckled heartily. When Whittingham shakily laid his glass on a side table to stop himself from spilling it as he continued to hoot with mirth, William turned a concerned face to Stephen. "I made a mistake, did I not?"

"You certainly… did not!" spluttered their companion through his guffaws. "But your mother was wrong. When in the company of *ladies* you should talk about the weather but not in a gentleman's club. God, you don't want to bore us to death. Tupping is acceptable in a gentleman's club but not around the older gentlemen. You don't want to make them jealous."

"Whittingham!" It was a warning shot. Whittingham was good fun and he was sure his friend had worked out exactly what was the issue with Oldbeck, and a bit of light teasing was fine. He just didn't want Harriet's brother ridiculed.

"Oldbeck knows I'm jesting. Your sister is right, man. Tupping is probably not the best discussion starter. A good rule of thumb, I always find is to let others start the conversation and find the topic, that way I stay out of the firing line. And that firing line is usually a hard swat on the arm with my mother's fan. And bloody hell can that woman hit. Thank Christ they don't teach women to fence. She would have me speared through the gut in seconds."

"I would like to learn to fence," said Oldbeck wistfully, his red eyebrows furrowing slightly. "And to dance."

"You do not know how to dance?" Stephen asked, slightly horrified. But then the boy had been schooled at home. Had no one foreseen this moment when he would take up his earldom and need to come into society? Poor Harriet. No wonder the chit was at her wits' end. And it really was not all because of Oldbeck's behaviour. He just needed training. She had been left with a mess to clear up and no relatives upon whom she could lean.

"No."

"Well, that is one thing we can sort easily enough. And we shall really need to get you some new clothes. Those are a tad out of fashion, and as for that waistcoat. Sorry, but you do look a bit of a dandy in it. Beau Brummel would be proud."

"I used to be a dandy," interjected Whittingham sulkily.

"Thank you for making my point for me. See, Oldbeck. You do not want to turn out like Whittingham. Imagine having Harriet whacking you at regular intervals with her fan."

Oldbeck laughed. His laugh was loud and deep—too loud for the weak joke that Stephen had made, but the man's face lit up and in that moment it was glaringly obvious that Oldbeck would be classed by society as an imbecile and would need protecting to some degree. The laugh had drawn a few haughty stares and Stephen stared straight back, daring comment or censure.

Stephen may be a nobody himself—the second son of a duke, being called lord merely as a courtesy but it made no difference. He would not let any gentleman, no matter his rank, look down their noses at a peer of the realm for laughing too loudly. They had all acted more foolishly than this when they were in their cups. They could help it, William could not.

When had Stephen become an advocate for the feeble-minded? He looked at Oldbeck who was gulping his wine, licking his lips and sitting back with a big grin plastered on his face. And he knew. He'd become an advocate of The Earl of Oldbeck when he had met him and realised he was a person who needed a little help to reach his full potential. Was there anything so wrong with that?

****

The next day Harriet, Mary and Phoebe sat in William's

study looking upon the severe countenance of Miss Prewitt, the second candidate for the position of governess. Harriet reckoned Miss Prewitt to be around forty years of age, the small amount of brown hair she could see under the bonnet beginning to go grey. It was clearly tied in a severe knot at the nape of her neck. Miss Prewitt had little lines around her mouth from puckering her lips in disapproval. They were quite indented at present.

Six-year-old Phoebe put a tiny cross on the piece of paper she had in front of her. Harriet smiled at the woman. The interview had not even started yet.

"I am Lady Harriet, the sister of the Earl of Oldbeck. This is Miss Callahan and this is Miss Charville, the niece of the Duke of Halimead. We have a slightly unusual request for the first few weeks of your employment and then it would be more regular duties."

"I do not want to work in a house where… funny business is going on."

Harriet gritted her teeth. Why did educated women always assume the aristocracy were all up to depraved acts? She doubted she would know a depraved act if it happened on the breakfast table in front of her. She was a woman of gentle birth and good breeding. Of course her feeble-minded brother had got the kitchen maid with child—but that aside, there was no funny business going on in the house and she was trying to rectify the aforementioned situation.

"Miss Callahan needs to be schooled in lady-like pursuits, comportment, how to behave like a lady in genteel company, suitable topics of conversation, dancing, perhaps singing and needlework. She is to marry my brother—the Earl of Oldbeck. The whys and wherefores of Miss Callahan's missed education are unimportant but she must be given this education as quickly as possible. Meanwhile. Miss Charville needs to begin her studies as soon as possible. I fear her father has had her in the nursery a little too long and she needs to learn to be more like a lady."

Harriet gave the little girl a tender smile and the child smiled up at her beatifically. Apart from the house party they had attended two summers ago, today was the first time she had met Phoebe. And they had got on well immediately.

The would-be governess's gaze swept over Mary, assessing her. Mary had complained about being primped and having her hair curled and twisted into the pretty style by a maid earlier that morning, but Harriet had insisted and it had been worth the effort. She looked every bit the gentle-born miss that Harriet was trying to convey to the world. Mary bit her lip, showing her unease at the scrutiny. Thankfully Mary was early enough on in her pregnancy that it did not show yet.

"Are you staying here, Miss Callahan?" asked the governess suddenly.

"Yes." Mary frowned and looked at Harriet to make sure she had given the correct answer."

"Then what of the earl?"

Harriet nodded her understanding of this line of questioning. Thank heavens that when Stephen and William had returned the night before, Stephen had taken charge and instilled a few rules and boundaries. Oldbeck would move in to Stephen's townhouse and learn to be a gentleman, thus not living under the same roof as his betrothed, chaperoned by only his spinster sister. And now she could look this woman in the eye and tell the truth. "He is staying with Lord Stephen, Phoebe's father. The Duke of Halimead's brother." Phoebe nodded wildly as if daring the woman to not believe her new friend.

"May I see your references?"

The woman handed over the papers. A quick glance through them told Harriet all she needed to know. She knew some of the women and girls to whom Miss Prewitt had been governess. They were all nasty little shrews without a sense of humour between them. Not one of them would ever give quarter to William because of his nature and they would all look down their noses at her entire family because he was different.

"Do you know anything about the Earl of Oldbeck, Miss Prewitt?"

"Know anything?"

The woman looked as if she was trying to hold something back. Harriet's laugh was an insincere tinkle, one she had used many times in ballrooms and drawing rooms when she was anything but sincere.

"Oh come now, Miss Prewitt. I am sure even you occasionally hear gossip or have occasion to check out Debrett's. My father died not eight months ago. There will be those who are scandalised that we only stayed in mourning for six months but honestly, he told us that we must not mourn for any longer. So I am sure you have heard of the earl and his… difficulties."

"I am sure I do not understand what you mean, my lady."

"I am sure you do, Miss Prewitt. Miss Callahan struggles with reading, writing and numbers, as does the earl. Will that be a problem?"

The woman's eyes flicked over Mary again, the lines on her mouth deepening again. "I am sure it shall not be a problem. If she can behave herself in polite company, that is."

Harriet looked at Mary. Beseeching eyes gazed back. *Please don't pick her*, they said.

"But, what if I am unable to behave in polite company?" asked Phoebe suddenly.

Mary guffawed, a loud raucous laugh, giving away herself for the first time. Too loud and a little out of place for that moment. Phoebe leaned over and gave Mary a conspiratorial smile.

"You are a child. You shall behave as you are told or you shall go to bed hungry."

"Perhaps Mary should go to bed hungry too if she does not behave as she ought," said Phoebe. Oh dear! How had this got so out of control? And then it got worse.

"Oh no. I could not go to bed hungry. It would be bad for the baby."

"The baby? What baby? I knew this was a house of sin."

Chapter Six

Harriet and Mary stood on the doorstep of Lord Stephen's townhouse at ten o'clock on Sunday morning. They were there to collect William for church.

The butler appeared, a scowl on his face. He clearly expected Harriet.

"I have come to collect the Earl of Oldbeck for church."

"Ah yes. Please come in, Lady Harriet. His lordship is um… nearly ready."

That was clearly a polite half truth. She could hear her brother shouting.

She walked past the butler and into the hallway. William's voice was coming from upstairs.

"It is too tight."

"Look," the lower, more measured tones of Stephen could just be heard, "we are not in the country now. When I took you to White's, we got away with you looking a bit scruffy, but you cannot go to church looking like you were dragged through a hedge backwards. Not only is it a disgrace to your family, to your name, to your poor sister, but it is an affront to God. Not to mention to your valet. What is your name?"

"Mason, my lord." Harriet recognised the voice of William's long-suffering man servant. She often wondered why the valet had stayed for so long. Though he had been in the employ of the Oldbeck estate for a many years.

"Mason. Well, from now on your work will be appreciated and the Earl of Oldbeck will allow you to tie his cravats appropriately. He will not remove them, nor will he loosen them. He will not complain. It will be the same with all of his clothes. He will allow you to have some pride in your work."

"But... But..."

"No buts, Oldbeck. You want respect, do you not? It starts with the servants. And that means you allow them to do their jobs properly. Now come, I heard the door. I believe Lady Harriet and Miss Callahan have arrived. Oldbeck, do not run!"

She heard his feet thundering down the stairs before she saw him, his hair still damp from his bath and curling around his collar. Mason and Lord Stephen had done a marvellous job in sprucing up her brother. He looked like any other gentleman of the *ton*, until he grabbed Mary into a less than genteel kiss.

"William!" Harriet cried out as she heard a pin from Mary's neat coiffure tinkle onto the black and white tiles.

"Oldbeck!" Lord Stephen's voice was a warning growl and William let go and stepped back.

"I apologise. I was excited."

Stephen reached the bottom step and bowed elegantly to the ladies.

"Lady Harriet, Miss Callahan, it is a pleasure to see you again."

"The pleasure is all ours, my lord," Harriet replied with a curtsey. Mary bobbed a curtsey alongside her. She was going to have to teach the girl a proper curtsey as opposed to a maid's curtsey, she supposed. And she would have to find out if Mary would need to curtsey in front of the King. She had no idea. Perhaps the patronesses of Almack's would know but then Harriet so seldom went to town, she doubted she would even be eligible for vouchers to Almack's. And once the news that her imbecile brother was marrying the maid he had impregnated was out then she doubted she would be deemed good enough to serve the punch in the hallowed halls of that establishment ever again.

"Lady Harriet?" She looked up into the most beautiful brown eyes and blushed at the look of concern in them. "Are you quite well?"

"Oh yes, I am very well. I was wool gathering. I apologise. We must go or we shall be late."

"I do wish I could go with you but I had promised my mother to accompany her today since my brother shall be in the country. But Phoebe and I are coming to your house for lunch after and then we are all going for a drive in the park, am I correct?"

"Yes. That was the general idea."

"And then the Simkins squeeze tonight."

"If we must."

"You do not sound particularly enthusiastic. I thought all young ladies enjoyed partying and the marriage mart in particular."

"These are hardly ideal circumstances. Besides, if you fail in your endeavours this week, I already have myself a husband. And if you succeed I shall be a maiden aunt I suspect. I shall paint watercolours or write Gothic novels or something."

"You could marry someone else… someone older who needs children to carry on their line."

"I could. But being a brood mare has little appeal to me."

They were at the door now.

"Oldbeck, remember you must pay attention to both your sister and Mary. You must not ignore Lady Harriet. You must call Mary 'Miss Callahan' at all times. You must not damage her reputation. No touching anything but her arm and if her glove is not on then you DO NOT TOUCH!" He leaned closer to the younger man and spoke very quietly but Harriet could still hear. "And if you have memories or thoughts of tupping her and it starts to get hard, start to count to fifty in twos. Two, four, six, eight, ten, twelve… just like that. It will go away and you shall forget."

Harriet blinked. Oh dear, she really wished she had not heard that. But she was a little fascinated by it too.

The butler offered William his hat and gloves and her brother put them on quickly before offering Harriet his arm. He'd obviously been told she must be escorted rather than Mary since she was the lady of higher rank. They walked out to the barouche and William helped both ladies into the carriage. Lord Stephen was walking down his front steps, Phoebe in tow, as William clambered in and took the seat opposite the ladies. He nodded his head and Phoebe waved before they turned down the street in the direction of the Halimead townhouse to meet his mother.

Harriet watched him go with a ridiculous sense of loss. There was something about him. She felt safe in his presence and a little as if a part of her was missing when he was away. But of course, that was silly. She hardly knew the man.

They rolled up to the church a few minutes later. The modern building was only a few streets away from their townhouse but with the detour to pick up William and the necessity to not be stopped and spoken to by half the *ton*, Harriet had just deemed it easier to take a carriage. Besides, most of the *ton* travelled around Mayfair in carriages despite the whole area being walking distance even including most of Hyde Park—if you had boots on and not silly slippers of course.

A number of members of the congregation were milling around outside, talking until it was time for the service to start. The day was grey but not wet or cold. A slight wind wafted the feathers in some of the ladies' bonnets and fluttered a few skirts, showing off the ladies' legs. Harriet was not sure how appropriate that was for the churchyard. William climbed down and helped first Harriet and then Mary alight from the barouche. They walked into the churchyard and stopped to exchange greetings with a few people whom Harriet knew from previous Seasons and trips to London.

They had just arrived at the door of the church when the vicar's wife approached. Harriet smiled warmly. Mrs Paton was a short, comely woman with twinkling blue eyes and greying hair held back in a tight, unforgiving bun. Her dress was made of grey wool with a pretty lace collar which Harriet suspected she made herself. Mary looked transfixed by the intricate design.

"Lord Oldbeck, Lady Harriet, it is a pleasure to see you in town again."

"Mrs Paton, may I introduce Miss Callahan, Lord Oldbeck's betrothed. She is new to town this season. Her parents have both passed away and I have taken it upon myself to introduce her to society myself."

Mary bobbed a curtsey as did Mrs Paton, who registered surprise at the young lady's subservience but masked it well. It was only then that Harriet noticed a problem. William was on his hands and knees. A young lady, standing near to the church wall, wrenched the hem of her gown out of William's hand then turned around and crouched down. Lifting up a gold coin, she smiled and handed it to him.

"William, stand up." Harriet whispered, looking around to see how many people had noticed. It seemed that some may be able to see William, but none could see the girl. "Quickly. Oh!"

"Stay there for a moment, Abigail," said the vicar's wife sternly moving her body slightly to hide the girl from sight. "Do not draw attention to yourself."

William got to his feet and dusted the dirt from his knees.

"I dropped my money for the offering." His face red and his eyes lowered. He knew he had done the wrong thing.

"William, you were…"

"Lady Harriet, I think it best we discuss this privately, do you not agree?"

Harriet looked around at the other members of the congregation and realised they were all filing into church—still unaware of what had just happened.

"Yes, of course."

"Perhaps we could talk after the service."

Harriet wanted to cry. She could feel the tears sting in the backs of her eyes but she had been taught not to cry. Young ladies do not cry in front of others. It is just not good *ton*.

"Yes, that would be fine." She hated that her voice had come out weak and broken.

"Before you go in, let me assure you that no harm has been done and Abigail's reputation will be fine. All anyone saw was your brother on his knees picking up something. Perhaps he was a little close to my ankles but he is unlikely to get much of a thrill from them and I assure you, my reputation is solid."

"Thank you."

"Well, I would prefer you to be concentrating on God than worrying about my wrath, my dear," said the older woman. "Come, the service is about to start."

****

An hour later Harriet, Mary, William, Mrs Paton, the Vicar and Abigail stood in the vestry.

"I am very sorry Vicar, Mrs Paton and Abigail, of course. I didn't mean to … well I don't know…. ruin Abigail… I mean Miss Paton." William was fidgeting with the fingers of his leather gloves, probably worrying a hole into them. Mason would not be pleased. Harriet could see that William wanted to pace. He was bouncing on his heels and his voice was getting higher in tone and volume.

"You have not ruined Miss Paton, Lord Oldbeck, though you may have, had it not been for Abigail's quick thinking," said her mother in a kind but slightly chastising manner. Harriet appreciated this. William needed to learn but he understood the gravity of this situation.

"You would have had to have married Abigail instead and what would have happened to the baby?" said Mary.

Harriet groaned internally.

"You are with child, Miss Callahan?" asked the vicar. Mary nodded and blushed looking at Harriet apologetically. "And you are going to do the right thing by her?" He speared William with a glare.

"The right thing?"

"Are you marrying her?"

"Yes. Of course. I love her." He looked at his fiancée and grinned, then his brow furrowed. She watched as his lips started moving. Oh no, Harriet realised her brother was counting in twos. She forced herself to look away. There was no way she was looking to see what state he was in.

The vicar's face broke into a smile.

"Will you be getting a special licence?"

"We will. We are getting Lord Oldbeck some help at polishing his skills—and Miss Callahan too. I wondered if you knew of any young ladies who may be interested in a governess post with a difference. You see, Lord Stephen Charville and I are working with Lord Oldbeck and Miss Callahan. Lord Stephen has a six-year-old daughter who really needs a governess and we thought that Miss Callahan could sit in on lessons for a few weeks. Our difficulty is finding someone who would be appropriate but would not…well… judge Miss Callahan for her upbringing and if they found out about her…" she rubbed her own stomach slightly "…state."

"Abigail is looking for work as a governess. She is twenty-one, has a good education and has read all the books on etiquette. We are a good middle-class family and have been in and around the *ton* all her life. We have brought her up to see the world through the eyes of Jesus

Christ. Judge not lest ye be judged."

At last Abigail walked forwards.

"Miss Callahan, it would be my pleasure to help you if you would allow me. And a six-year-old girl sounds like a delight for a first charge. I would promise to continue my own studies from your library if you would allow me access. I believe that continuing to learn is the most important thing a governess can do."

"Well it is not just my decision to make but I would be happy to employ you as governess, Miss Paton. Would you and Mrs Paton please come to Oldbeck House tomorrow afternoon at three o'clock to meet Lord Stephen and we can make a final decision?"

"Oh that would be wonderful."

The young woman's green eyes lit up with excitement and Harriet could see it took all her strength of will not to jump up and down. Her mother and father looked at each other, a satisfied look on their faces. It seemed it had been a good day all round. They needed a governess and her family had known the Patons for years. Her father had spoken well of the Reverend Paton. It looked as if disaster had been averted and good had come out of a near travesty. She just had to convince Lord Stephen that Miss Paton would make a good governess.

Chapter Seven

"It is raining." Phoebe scowled as she craned her neck to see out of the long windows at the rear of Oldbeck House. They were eating a sumptuous Sunday lunch of turkey and beef. Phoebe had been allowed to join the grown-ups as the nursery in Oldbeck House was in disrepair. The schoolroom was currently being put back to rights for when a suitable governess could be appointed.

"So it is." Stephen looked out of the window and saw that indeed it was raining and quite heavily too. "Well, at least Hyde Park will be quiet for our ride."

"We cannot go for a drive in this weather," exclaimed the little girl.

"Why ever not?" he teased. They always played this game.

"Because we shall all catch chills and die."

"Well that's rather dramatic. More likely we shall catch chills, be slightly unwell and recover fully, but yes, best not to take any chances I suppose."

"So do we have to stay in all afternoon?" whined Oldbeck.

"Gentlemen do not whine," Stephen admonished. "Besides, complaining about English weather is futile. Let us be honest, it rains all the time in England. It is a fact of life."

"But what shall we do?"

"We shall do what we always do when it rains, William.

We shall read and write letters and play cards and charades and other parlour games."

"You know I cannot read or write letters. And parlour games are tiresome. I hate the rain."

"Perhaps I could read," said Lord Stephen jovially. "Do you know Robinson Crusoe, Oldbeck?"

"Can't say I do. Is he a nice chap?"

"It is a book. It is a story of a young chap who goes to sea against his parents' wishes."

"Oh, we may as well listen then," said William, waving his hand dismissively and getting up. "Much better than playing stuffy old parlour games with Harry."

"I shall get our copy form the library. It was one of Papa's favourites. But he never read aloud to us," said Harriet, pulling herself to her feet, looking somewhat weary and defeated. Stephen tried to give her an encouraging smile and when her green eyes lit up slightly, he felt a jolt of awareness in his breeches. He liked easing her burden it seemed. If he was not careful, he would soon be counting in twos…

****

Five minutes later they were all seated around the hearth in the drawing room and Lord Stephen started the story of the contrary young man, Robinson Crusoe. Of course, Harriet had read the book in her childhood and had enjoyed it, but it seemed that no one had thought to read the tale to her younger brother. She wondered why she never had. And why had neither of her parents or the nanny or tutors? Perhaps Robinson was seen as a bad influence on a boy such as William.

Stephen's dulcet baritone voice was perfect as he described Robinson's parents' concerns about their son going to sea and his first voyage. She enjoyed watching her brother's face change as Robinson first hated the sea voyage, then loved it, then got drunk, then began to fear for his life again, before getting drunk yet again. She had a feeling that William may very well have chosen to come home at that point, proving that despite him being classed as an imbecile, he was possibly more sensible than a lot of young men.

Lord Stephen read until Robinson was captured by pirates. A look of amusement crossing his face as he closed the leather bound volume. She looked at her soon-to-be sister-in-law who sat enraptured staring into nothingness and then to her brother, the excitement evident on his face. Disappointment flashed across William's features, but Harriet could not help thinking he held his tongue for fear his new friend would refuse to read from the book at a later date if he made a fuss. As she turned to Lord Stephen he caught her gaze and grinned. Phoebe was nestled against his side, drowsy from the heat of the fire but aware her father had finished his reading.

"Papa, are you not going to read more?"

"No, my darling, not today. Perhaps another day. There are other things we can do on a Sunday afternoon. We could be scandalous and have dancing lessons. Lord Oldbeck says that he does not know how to dance. I think it is time he was taught."

"Ooh yes, let's." said Mary, jumping to her feet.

Harriet hid a smile behind her handkerchief.

"Oh I was only teasing."

"I think that is what they mean when they say one is hoist by their own petard, Lord Stephen." She could not help it. He looked vaguely horrified. "Oh come on. It would only be a little dancing with the family and one of the maids playing the pianoforte. No one would know. Besides, it is not as if we are Presbyterians. I promise not to allow the maid to play a waltz."

He guffawed at that.

"So we are going to be dancing?" said Phoebe, wriggling free from her father.

"Yes," Harriet said decisively. "But first we shall have

tea."

She got up to ring for the bell just as Lord Stephen got up to move seats. They found themselves, quite by accident, toe to toe, forehead to chin.

"I do beg your pardon, my lord," she whispered, stepping to the side. Unfortunately, in an attempt to get out to the awkward situation they were in, Lord Stephen stepped to the same side.

His nearness seemed to set her off balance and muddle her thoughts. All she could do was breathe in the scent of him. It was a musky scent—spicy and very male. She stared at his emerald cravat pin which sat right at her eye level. She dared not look up into his eyes. Those chocolate depths that stole her very soul. He'd not had this effect on her two years ago. He had just vexed her with his need to mollycoddle her after a quick dip in the pond.

Lord Stephen reached out a hand, pulled the bell cord for a servant then took her by the shoulders and turned her round. Guiding her back towards her chaise.

"It looked like you and Lord Stephen were going to kiss there," said William—subtle as a coach and six as ever.

"Only if she was going to kiss his cravat, dummy," said Mary.

"Don't call me a dummy. I meant they were so close and Harry's cheeks are all red now. I think she likes him."

"Oh she does," agreed Mary.

Oh God, she wanted to die. Now.

Chapter Eight

William helped Harriet down from the coach and Lord Stephen helped Miss Callahan down. The gentlemen escorted the ladies inside the Simkins London residence. They had waited at least half an hour for their carriage to make it to the head of the line so they could alight and enter the house. Once inside Harriet heard Lord Stephen's murmured directions to Miss Callahan as to what to do, his instructions polite and subtle. She would be introduced as William's intended for the first time and was under strict instructions to do and say as little as possible to draw attention to herself. As a maid for many years in a big house, they had decided that Mary could probably pull that off quite easily. It was, after all, the job of staff to be not seen or heard.

Once they had been introduced by a footman, something that had caused a few murmurings—no doubt from people wondering who Miss Callahan was—the gentlemen went in one direction and the ladies in another. They were approached by the Countess of Assynt and her two twittering daughters. The woman wore a garish turban with three large peacock feathers, while her earlobes were weighed down with the heaviest diamonds that Harriet had ever seen—and Harriet had seen a lot of diamonds in her life. The daughters were typical young ladies in white silk gowns, searching for husbands and probably failing due to their overbearing mother.

"Ah Lady Harriet, I hear you brought your... err... brother with you. I hope he is going to behave himself."

"I am sure he will," Harriet answered politely, seething inwardly. "Pray, how is Viscount Hornby and his lovely wife? Does she still sing in the opera? Or has motherhood stopped her? I have to say everyone was surprised how healthy the baby was when it was born at just six months. Such a blessing though for you."

"Oh yes, it is and they are all doing fine, thank you. Oh I beg your pardon. I see Lady Stanhope. I must speak to her. Lovely chatting."

As the woman rushed away, Mary turned to Harriet.

"Lady Harriet, that was a bit cruel. They will say that about me."

"Mayhap, my dear, but I shall not be the one sticking the knife in first."

"Oh I see." Though Harriet suspected she did not. But the thing was, the *ton* was a nasty institution, if one could call it an institution. One had to have claws to survive it, especially when one's brother was classed as an imbecile... and that was one of the more pleasant epithets used for William.

"Ah Lady Harriet, how lovely to see you." A gentleman bowed courteously to Harriet and she curtseyed to him.

"Lord Dansworth, always a pleasure. May I introduce Miss Callahan? She is to marry the Earl of Oldbeck."

Lord Dansworth bowed to Mary. She curtseyed slowly as Harriet had taught her earlier that afternoon after their impromptu dance lesson. She was a fast learner, at least in this instance.

"A pleasure, Miss Callahan. May I say you look very fetching this evening? Perhaps you might honour me with this dance."

"Oh I..."

"What Miss Callahan means is that she turned her ankle on her way out of church this morning and it still pains her. She would be too polite to refuse you as she does not know you, my lord, but as old friends, I have no such compunctions. If I may, I shall refuse you on her behalf and you can be offended at my rudeness."

He chortled merrily.

"Same old Harry, eh? What about you, then. Would you dance with me?"

"I would love to but I would not wish to leave Miss Callahan alone."

"Let us look after Miss Callahan then." Harriet turned to see Lord Stephen and William standing, glasses of champagne in hand. "Please, go ahead and dance."

Harriet smiled and accepted Lord Dansworth's hand graciously. She had not really wanted to dance but it would be churlish to refuse now—not to mention impolite.

It was a waltz and that meant she would have to speak to him throughout the dance. That may be a problem.

"So Oldbeck is getting a leg shackle, is he?"

"Yes, he is."

Dansworth began to sweep her expertly around the floor. He was, like most gentlemen of the *ton*, an excellent dancer.

"He is not... how shall I say it... the marrying type?"

"Because he's an imbecile?"

"Now, I never said that, Harry."

"That is Lady Harriet to you. And you did not have to say it, my lord. I know what everyone is thinking."

"Do you?"

"Yes, I do, as it happens, for I would be thinking the same thing."

"Is she marrying him for the money?"

"No. Believe it or not, it is a love match."

"A love match?"

"Yes. They happen. Do you think my brother would marry for anything less?" They stopped talking as Dansworth navigated them through a crush of bodies. When they eventually reached something approximating fresh air again, Dansworth spoke.

"Probably not. But will she be happy with someone like Oldbeck?"

"She is like Oldbeck. She has difficulty with words and numbers and understanding too."

His lips formed an 'o' shape.

"But what about children? Will they not be like their parents?"

"There is no telling. They think that the reason William has problems is because my mother had difficulties birthing him. She nearly died. Why Miss Callahan is the way she is, one cannot tell. She has no parents to ask. But James, we are old friends, please, I beg you, do not gossip about this. There shall be enough gossip and, whereas I do not care so much for I have given up all hope of marriage and care not for the good graces of the *Beau Monde*, I do fear for William who shall have to come to town frequently. Lord Stephen Charville is helping him, but this is a cruel world. You know this."

Dansworth smiled kindly and squeezed her hand gently.

"Do not concern yourself, Harry. I shall not breathe a word to anyone. Not even my mistress."

"Oh you are such a rake."

"Indeed. Ah this dance is over and it is with sadness but with a little relief that I return you to Charville's side because he looks like he wants to call me out and I do not think I could beat him in a duel. I am told he is a sharp shooter with a pistol. I do believe the fellow is jealous."

"Jealous? Oh, I do not believe so."

****

When Lady Harriet arrived back at Stephen's side, Dansworth bowed and took his leave. She was flushed and smiling. He did not like it one little bit. He had watched her conversing amicably with Dansworth as they waltzed. The man was a known rake.

His hand had been a little too low on Lady Harriet's back to be appropriate. Then he had looked up and grinned at Stephen as if baiting him. Little did Dansworth realise that Stephen was not the slightest bit interested in Lady Harriet. Oh she was beautiful, clever, witty, intelligent, adorable and was filling out her ball gown exquisitely. But he was sworn off marriage altogether.

Harriet was looking around the ballroom, an anxious expression on her face.

"Lord Stephen, where are my brother and his betrothed?"

"Over at the punch bowl." Stephen had sent them over a couple of minutes earlier to stop William prattling about how great it all was and how many candles there must be in the chandeliers. It had not been well done of him but he'd been so annoyed by the proprietorial way Dansworth had been holding his Harriet.

She stood on tiptoe to see the refreshments table.

"No, they are not. They are not there, my lord." Her voice was higher than normal—slightly panicked.

Stephen turned, noted too they were not there then did a quick scan of the room.

"Devil take it. Come with me." He caught Harriet by the elbow. A young man and his lady. There was only one place he would take her and that was the balcony. He only had to hope they got there before a scandal occurred. William had no sense of propriety.

Stephen did not care that people may think they were hurrying out for an assignation of their own. If he had to marry the chit to save her reputation, then so be it. At the moment, he had to stop Oldbeck from cocking everything up. As they walked through the double doors he found Elizabeth and his brother standing talking to Oldbeck and Miss Callahan. They approached slowly so as to pretend nothing was out of the ordinary.

Elizabeth turned.

"Ah Lord Stephen, darling, I hear that you may be

employing a governess for our niece. About time too. Miss Callahan was telling us all about it."

"She was?" Harriet looked appalled.

The duchess turned to Harriet and smiled graciously

"The story seems a little disjointed and she has turned a delightful shade of pink a few times and stopped talking so I suspect it to be somewhat edited. Please do not worry, Lady Harriet, I have a sister who has similar qualities to Miss Callahan and your brother. She gets up to all kinds of mischief. Even if I were to learn of the whole story, I am sure I would not be shocked. Melissa has probably done worse."

Harriet appeared to relax somewhat and drew in a deep breath.

"You look a little overset, if you do not mind me saying, Lady Harriet," said the Duke of Halimead.

"Your Graces, I am sorry I…" She curtseyed low, obviously realising she had not done so when she had met them.

"Oh my dear, please, while we appreciate the gesture, it is not necessary when you were clearly worried for your brother. As you can see, he and his young lady are fine. Perhaps we could chaperone them. My brother could escort you for a while and allow you to get some fresh air on this lovely balcony."

"That would be lovely. If Lord Stephen does not mind."

"Oh Lord Stephen does not mind," chimed in the duchess. "He loves a walk in the gardens as much as the next gentleman." She gave her husband a knowing look who returned a warning glance before ushering their charges back through the French doors.

Stephen did not mind at all. He liked Lady Harriet and enjoyed her company. It was nice to have five minutes with her where they did not have to worry about William or Mary or Phoebe. He glanced back at where his sister-in-law and brother had been, wondering why the devil they were here and not in the country but that could wait. For now he could turn his attention to Lady Harriet.

They walked down the steps of the balcony into the garden which was lit with strings of lanterns.

"Thank you for arranging dresses for Phoebe. You sent the bills to me?"

"I did. The Oldbeck estate is barely turning a profit at present. I am afraid I am past the point of pride and could not have afforded to clothe someone else's child when I have just bought a wardrobe for Mary. You should have someone on your staff who can alter her gowns though. It is worth enquiring of your housekeeper. Your governess will be able to take her for new gowns once you have one in place. You should not be bothered with such tasks in the future."

"Lizzie, the duchess, usually does that but she was supposed to be going back to country. Presumably they have been delayed or something."

"You seem a little put out that she is here."

"No, not as such. I just wonder if she was telling me the truth when she said she was going back to the country or if she was trying to make me responsible for Phoebe."

"She is your daughter."

"I know." Anger rose in him. "Why does everyone think I am a useless father to her? I am doing my best."

She turned and cupped his cheek—a forward gesture that took him by surprise.

"No one thinks you are useless. But fathers sometimes forget what daughters need. I know my father did."

"And what do daughters need?"

His voice rasped. Her closeness set him on edge, but not in a bad way. He watched her red lips open as she started to speak.

"Love, companionship, tenderness, care, protection."

"Are these not the things a lover needs?"

"Perhaps."

He lowered his head so their lips were but an inch

apart.

"And what does Harriet need?"

He heard her swallow hard, but she looked up into his eyes and her lips parted slightly. He was torn between pushing her away and enveloping her in his embrace. How had he got himself into such a situation?

"Help. With William and Mary. And not just for a week."

"Do you still want me to marry you?"

"Yes." Her voice was a whisper.

"And what about when I come to take my conjugal rights, Harriet?"

Another swallow. Then that pretty pink tongue darted out to wet her red lips. He felt his breeches tighten. Damn, this was dangerous territory.

"There is nothing to fear. Every woman must accept a man into her bed at some point. Some even enjoy it."

"And would you enjoy it, Harriet? My hands roaming all over your bare flesh, the weight of my body atop yours, my sweat dripping onto you as I rut above you, my lips crushing yours?"

He placed his hand on the back of her head, expecting her to pull away but she did not.

When he captured her lips roughly, she grabbed his shoulders. Pushing his tongue into her mouth, he claimed her, moving her against a tree for support. He angled her head, his fingers digging though her neat coiffure to position her the way he wanted her, as his tongue rasped along hers, his lips giving her no quarter. A muffled gasp as she tried to comprehend his roughness, a movement of her breasts against his chest as she lifted herself to meet him more fully. Good God, despite his manhandling, she was enjoying this.

He cupped her breast, hoping it would make her see sense. When his thumb flicked over the distended peak hidden under layers of clothing, she made a little noise of pleasure in the back of her throat. A beautiful throat that was now extended and needing to be kissed. He pressed light kisses down the narrow column, towards her chest, then back up before he travelled into very dangerous territory. Along her jaw line he peppered little kisses before capturing her mouth, this time tenderly, the way he should have done the first time. The way a lady should be kissed.

She melted into him, both arms around his neck, kissing him back as if her very life depended on it, her tongue matching his, stroke for stroke, tentatively at first, then more boldly.

One of her hands moved over off his shoulder and under his coat, exploring. Her gloved palm rested on his waistcoat over his heart which appeared to be trying to leap out of his chest. He moved his head, kissing her deeper still, eliciting another little pleasure noise from her. He wondered what noises she would make when his tongue moved over her… But no! She was an innocent and this was already too far.

He tried to draw away but her hand held his head in place as she continued her tongue's explorations. He could not bring himself to wrench himself away from her. When her hand on his chest moved lower, around his waist on onto his arse, he nearly stopped breathing. Harriet was delightfully innocent and wonderfully curious. She had no understanding of the power of her own sexuality, just as Sarah had not in the beginning. Thoughts of Sarah made him more determined to pull away from the embrace this time. Sarah had been the last woman he had kissed and the last woman he had made love to.

He turned his head slightly and Harriet's lips grazed the side of his mouth, then his cheek. A little whine of displeasure came from her and he moved her head onto his chest, trying not to reject her out of hand but to cool the heat of their passionate embrace.

"Harriet, we are at a *ton* entertainment. Anyone could catch us."

"Oh!"

He pressed his lips to the top of her head. He no more wanted to end this encounter than Harriet did. It had been six years since he'd had a woman in his arms. He had forgotten how right it felt—how necessary. He barely went out into company, so he was barely entranced by the fairer sex. On the odd occasion lust got the better of him, he had a right hand to sort out the necessary in the privacy of his bedchamber. But now, with this soft, fragrant creature rubbing her cheek against his waistcoat, catching her breath, he could not understand how he had survived this long.

"Let me see you and check your hair," he said. Harriet lifted her head and took a step back. He tilted his head and considered her coiffure before catching one stray curl that seemed to come from the middle of the part that was swept up. "I think this bit needs pinned up again," he said. "But otherwise, your style seems undamaged."

Harriet took the lock of hair and, biting her lip, fidgeted with one section of her hair for a minute before triumphantly looking up at him.

"Is it still falling down?"

"Not that I can see."

"Fine. How do I look?"

He adjusted the shoulders of her gown and swept his gaze over her. "Your lips are a little swollen. I guess people will think we have been kissing."

"Oh then we may make it into the scandal sheets."

"Perhaps. I thought you did not want to marry anyway."

"I am marrying you."

"Perhaps."

"There is no perhaps about it, Stephen. May I call you Stephen? I have had my hand on your posterior."

Stephen coughed to hide his bark of laughter. The chit was incorrigible.

"I suppose you may as well. May I call you Harriet?

"You may. If you are a gentleman, and you claim to be

one, then you will marry me as a reward for saving Phoebe. You did say anything. So gossip in the scandal sheets is immaterial."

And with that, she turned around and swept back up the garden path, leaving Stephen with no other option but to hurry after her and catch her arm so he could accompany her back inside the ballroom where everyone could see them and draw their own conclusions.

Chapter Nine

Harriet looked up as William barged into the breakfast room the next morning, loudly explaining to the butler that he did not need to be announced in his own house. He was followed by a skipping Phoebe and a disgruntled-looking second son of a duke.

"Lord Oldbeck, Miss Charville, Lord Stephen, good morning," said Harriet politely, pasting a polite smile on her face and indicating to the footman to bring up more tea and toast. "Please sit and join us. Have a cup of tea at least."

"Can I have breakfast, Harry? Charville is in a foul temper. Something to do with you in the scandal sheets and he dragged me here before I could get my ham and eggs."

She turned a bright smile to her brother.

"Of course you can. This is your house, after all. Just because you are staying with Lord Stephen temporarily does not mean we would starve you."

"You are in the scandal sheet? Is that because you and Lord Stephen were kissing in the garden?" asked Mary.

"You and Papa were kissing?" Phoebe looked from Harriet to her father, her little nose scrunched up and a look of sheer disgust on her face. "Why do grown-ups do that? It's horrible."

"Good God, we did not kiss," shouted Stephen throwing himself onto the dining room chair beside

Harriet. "The scandal sheet is wrong as usual."

Harriet placed her cup on her saucer.

"Phoebe, did your father ensure you had breakfast or are you hungry too?"

Phoebe looked at her father and bit her lip, obviously unwilling to rat out her beloved papa. Harriet nodded and rose to collect a plate. She placed a couple of slices of toast, some ham and a poached egg on the child's plate. She moved to turn back to the table but met with a wall of male chest.

"I apologise."

"For what? Lying or blaspheming at my breakfast table, my lord?" she hissed.

"Both?"

"You did not seem particularly sorry when you were…" She drew in a deep breath, remembering where she was and that she had an audience who were all agog. Luckily, she was good at whispering. "Oh never mind. I do not accept your apology, simply because it seems less than heartfelt. You do not even seem to know what you are apologising for."

"Well I think Lord Stephen did kiss Lady Harriet last night. Her hair was all mussed at the back when they returned from the garden," said Mary, giving William a knowing look.

"Maybe they did more than kiss," said William.

"That is enough!" cried Harriet, her voice just short of a screech. She drew in yet another deep breath, regained her composure and looked from her brother to his fiancée. "This is the breakfast table, there is a child present and we are polite company. Could we please refrain from discussing kissing or anything else that would carry on from such an act? It is not appropriate."

"Kissing is horrible anyway," said Phoebe, as Harriet laid the plate of food before her.

"I quite agree," said Harriet.

"You didn't agree last night," came a low rumble in her

ear. It took a mere two seconds and she could easily have missed the soft caress of a thumb across the exposed flesh of her neck, but she knew she had not when Stephen picked up his knife and fork and began to tuck into ham and eggs.

Why was every nerve in her body alive? And why was a man who maintained he did not want to marry her intent on vexing her in such a manner? She wanted to climb onto his knee, straddling him and then… what? Well she did not actually know but something told her that it would be pleasurable and that Stephen would know what to do.

****

"Well Miss Paton will make a wonderful addition to our staff, I believe. She seems bright, willing and more than able to keep both Phoebe and Mary in line. Hopefully she will be able to teach Mary appropriate dinner conversation and quickly."

He hoped so. He didn't need another meal that went along the lines of breakfast. He had wanted to kill someone by the end of it.

"It is hardly Mary's fault that she says what she sees. My hair was a mess when I returned from the garden last night."

"And whose fault is that?"

"You kissed me, my lord."

"You did not object, my lady." Oh he was a cad putting all this on her, but how was a man supposed to have resisted?

"Why should I?"

"To protect your reputation."

"What reputation? The spinster sister of an imbecile? Why do you think I am not married, Stephen? People are concerned it runs in the family. They do not want to take the chance that my first-born will be like William. I am no use to a first son. I am not even much use to a spare like yourself."

"Do not speak of yourself like that." Why did she always put herself down? And why did she shine such a harsh light on the ways of the *ton*? He was no fan of society, for sure but it had its place and he understood it. It was part of the reason he shunned it. And he was comfortable with his decision.

"Like what? Oh come now, Stephen. We all know that women are nothing more than brood mares. Your sister-in-law has not produced the heir to your brother's title yet. Are you not being pressured to marry and produce sons just in case?"

"No. And as for Elizabeth. Please do not speak of her in that manner. She has had a difficult time."

"I apologise. I do not mean to speak out of turn. I mean only to remind you of the realities of the situation, and that you have duties too. But any children we have are unlikely to be like my brother. I doubt even his children will be like him. And that is another reason he needs close family around him. So that his children can have people around them to help them learn to read and show them the ways of society when it is time. That is why we must marry. And that is why I will not allow you to distract me from this course of action."

Stephen was sat on the high-backed chair next to the hearth and gestured for her to take the other one. They were in the library of Oldbeck House having just interviewed and agreed employment terms with Miss Paton. Harriet shook her head.

She began to pace.

He loved watching ladies walk in their thin muslin gowns. Not much was left to the imagination—the way the fabric clung to their legs and hips. And Harriet was no exception. He could feel heat gathering under his cravat.

Devil take it.

Suddenly she stalked over to him and plonked herself down on his lap. He was so taken aback he could do nothing but wrap an arm around her waist to steady her.

She tugged at the shoulder of her gown, exposing more creamy flesh. But when she met with resistance from the fabric, she glowered at it then sighed.

"Harriet?"

She pressed her lips to his, lifting his hand and placing it on her breast.

He was a bit unsure how to respond, though he knew what he wanted to do. But want and should were two very different things and they were waging war within him. His mind told him it was wrong but his body was more than happy to let this take its course. He had an innocent throwing herself, rather ineptly, at him and he knew he had to tread very carefully.

"Do I need to pull the drapes?" she said, pulling her mouth away from his. "I suppose this should be done in the dark. And you shall have to help with the buttons of my gown."

"Forget the drapes." He tugged her against his chest, straightening her gown and pressing a kiss to her forehead. She snuggled against him.

"I did it wrong," she said, her voice defeated.

"No, not wrong. Just at the wrong moment."

"You do not want to… tup… me?"

"Is that what you want, Harriet? To be taken on a chair in the library? To be tupped like a kitchen maid? Is that what you think you are worth?"

"I…I…"

He fingered the top button of her gown then tweaked it open, then the next. She was still in his arms and he wondered if she was even breathing. Was she excited or fearful? He could not tell.

"Harriet, is this what you want?"

"You know what I want."

"For me to marry you."

"Yes."

"And all that entails."

She was silent for a moment and he thought she may be having second thoughts.

"Is it very wanton of me to say that I enjoyed our kisses last night? And the way you touched me? And the hardness of your body against mine?"

Stephen was embarrassed by the noise that came out of his throat as he moved Harriet forward to look into her eyes—to reassure her. It was half chuckle, half needy growl. God, he wanted her—badly.

"Harriet, it is not at all wanton to enjoy kissing or exploring one another's bodies. Even though we are not married. It is natural, especially for an innocent. Goodness, I am no innocent but I want to explore your body very much." He pushed her fischu out of the way slightly and pressed his lips to the rise of her breast. "I want to know what shade of pink your nipples are. I want to know if they are big or small. I want to know whether you prefer me to kiss, suck or lick them. And it is in these moments I am tempted to capitulate and agree to marry you, Lady Harriet. I am led by my manhood and my desire to see your breasts. Does that not make me the most fickle creature on God's green earth?"

"I must admit to being rather curious about what you look like naked. Thus if you are fickle, I must be fickle also."

"Ah but you have other reasons for marrying me. Loftier reasons."

"But you would be fulfilling your promise to me if you marry me."

"Perhaps."

"Are you going to tup me today?"

She was biting her lower lip, awaiting his reply, a mixture of excitement and fear in her gaze.

He tugged a few more buttons of her gown open and pressed his lips to her shoulder.

"No, my love, but I do want to see and feel a little more of you. Come." He stood, moving Harriet to her feet and walked to the desk. Stephen urged her to set her bottom to the edge of the mahogany top then he pressed his lips to hers, kissing her softly, coaxing her to follow his lead.

Soon, her arms were around his neck, her fingers burrowing under the back of his waistcoat. He pushed her gown up her thighs until there was enough width to allow him to move between her legs, place his hands on her pert backside and pull her against his hardening flesh. She felt good. She felt as though she was made to be there. He moved his mouth to kiss his way along her jaw and down the column of her neck. He nipped her shoulder, drawing a moan from her and a little thrust of her hips. Oh, Harriet Weatherby was going to be a wonderful, exciting and cooperative bed-partner. He tweaked her nipple and she sucked in a breath. And it was not a good sound. He lifted his head.

"Your courses are due?"

Her cheeks flushed a deep red.

"I do not think that is a suitable…"

Stephen pressed a finger to her lips to silence her.

"I have been married. My wife, Sarah—she always had tender breasts the day or two before her courses. Unless you are with child of course." His lips turned up in a teasing smile and she opened her mouth to protest until she noticed his expression.

"You brute," she grumbled.

"A brute you would have allowed you to undress you and would have made love to you on this desk, no doubt. But I have not agreed to marry you, Harriet. And I do not make a habit of debauching innocents, tempting though you may be."

"You were never going to…" she moved her hands as if unsure which euphemism to use. "Take my innocence?"

"No. I already said I would not."

"Then what was this? I thought I had enticed you. I thought you had changed your mind."

Stephen ran his fingers through his overly-long hair and stared at her. Her hair was beginning to fall out of its pins, her gown was half buttoned, her skin reddened by his rough chin.

"I do not know, Harriet. I…" He started to pace. "Since Sarah died things have been grey. It is the only way to describe it. Please do not misunderstand me. I love Phoebe. She is the one piece of sunshine in my life but we do not fully connect. I do not understand girls. Gowns and bonnets and stuff. What the hell do I know about such things? And so despite loving her with all my heart, nothing really has captured my attention. Then you came along. And you brought William and Mary. And by God, it has only been three days but it has been a jolly jape, has it not? I wish I had come to church with you. Taking William to White's was fun. The site of all those stuffy old lords when William laughed too loudly and spoke about tupping his lass. It is as if you and your family have brought colour to our lives. Phoebe and I can breathe and see and enjoy life.

And yes, Harriet. I have not touched a woman since Sarah died and I want to touch you. I want to undress you and feel you beneath me and sink into you.

But is that enough to marry you? I am a sullen old bugger. I was until three days ago at least. I do not want to saddle you with that. I worry this is just a short-term thing and I shall go back to being a misery and seeing life in shades of grey and you shall be stuck with me for life. Harriet, you're too good for that. You are too vibrant and colourful and full of life for that.

So to answer your question. This was about me stealing a little something of you without compromising you too much. As a gentleman, I apologise. As a man, I make no apologies and only wish I could have debauched you on the desk."

Harriet had stood throughout his speech and listened. She then smoothed the skirt of her gown and presented the little buttons at the back for him to do up. He felt awful. She must hate him now.

Then she turned around, cupped his cheek and pressed a soft kiss to his lips.

"They are so big…" She drew a circle about an inch and a half diameter over her breast. "And a dark rose colour, I suppose. Now, I think we should all go to Gunther's this afternoon for an ice. I really want one. I do not understand why, but I always want an ice the day before… Well, you know what I mean. And I have a feeling I may be staying abed tomorrow with a headache."

He grinned.

"Gunther's it is."

Chapter Ten

Harriet was feeling miserable. She turned onto her side and faced the door, listening to the sounds of the house as everyone prepared to leave for the Dowager Duchess of Halimead's Garden Party. Stephen's mother's entertainment was going to be a grand affair and she was stuck in bed, her stomach cramping so badly that it made her feel sick. Worst of all, Stephen knew why she was abed. When they'd had that encounter in the library and he had touched her breast, she had winced and he had worked it out. How terribly embarrassing.

Embarrassment washed over her again. In the far reaches of her mind, she knew she should not feel shame and that this was just a natural part of being a woman. But it was so messy and undignified and painful... for her at least. At her finishing school, some of her friends had no pain at all and stayed abed just a day for the worst of the bleeding to pass. Some poor girls were abed for almost a week. Harriet in some ways counted herself lucky. She was usually only abed for two days and the pain was, for the most part, tolerable. Some months it was worse than others. And she refused to have her mind addled with laudanum.

But for now she was in too much pain to read and that was annoying. She moaned into her pillow and muttered an unladylike profanity.

She heard the snick of the door and expected to see a

maid. Instead, Lord Stephen, hurried in, locked the door and stood, back to the door as if he had just broken in, which she supposed he had, in a way.

She yelped, pulling her covers up to her neck as she scrambled to sit up.

"Lord Stephen, you cannot be in my bedchamber."

"And yet I am."

"It is most improper."

"Yes, it is. But so is you sitting yourself on my lap in the library." He turned a wolfish smile on her. She inched closer to the centre of the bed as he advanced on her. He didn't mean to... Not here... Not when she had her courses.

"My Lord, I beg you, come no closer."

He stopped, scowling and ran his fingers through his hair.

"Harriet, I was only teasing. Do you really think I would hurt you? I brought you a couple of things. I know I should not be here but... I used to sneak into Sarah's bedchamber when she had... umm... her headaches... to cheer her up. She used to be miserable and look forward to it. I am sorry. I should go. You are not Sarah. I was not thinking clearly."

Harriet's heart seemed to be beating in her throat. There was certainly a huge lump as she looked at his big brown doleful eyes. He looked like a dog who had just been kicked.

"What did you bring me?"

He was just turning, but he swivelled on his heel—his expression changing as fast as lightning, back to the wolfish grin.

"So my lady, you are only interested in my visit for the gifts I bring."

Harriet adjusted the bedclothes so that they lay smoothly across her chest and waist, her legs now straight against the mattress.

"Until you agree to marry me, my lord, I see no other

reason to allow you into my bedchamber."

"Ah I see." He sat down on the edge of the bed without waiting for an invitation. Harriet could feel her cheeks burning with embarrassment and excitement. He lifted a hand and cupped her cheek, his cool touch soothing the warmth of her discomfiture. "Beautiful Harriet, do not look so afraid." He placed a book on his lap then dug into his coat pocket and produced a little jar of some kind of balm. "Rub it on your belly between your navel and your… uh… lower hairline, shall we say. It will soothe any pain though it will not take it away entirely. You may find you need it rubbed on your back. Do not put it any lower and wash your hands afterwards. There are chillies is in and it will hurt badly if you touch your eyes or other sensitive body parts while it is on your hands." He looked meaningfully at her lap and Harriet bit her lip. She understood which body part he meant.

"Thank you," she said, not sure how to recover from this intimate conversation despite the fact nothing much had been said.

"It always helped Sarah's headaches."

"Ah yes. I can see it having a curative effect on one's head."

"Quite."

"What else did you bring me?"

"A book?"

"An interesting book?"

"Probably not. You have probably read it. But I had no idea what else to bring."

He held out the spine to her.

"Northanger Abbey," she read. "Oh I do like Jane Austen."

"But you have read it?"

"I have. But I am happy to read it again. I must say though, Lord Stephen, I expected something more daring from you."

"More daring. Such as?"

"Oh I do not know... Fanny Hill perhaps."

"Fanny Hill? Pray tell, how does a gently bred daughter of an earl even know of such a book?"

"Oh come now, Lord Stephen, what do you think young ladies do at finishing school?"

"I thought you learned manners and how to snare a husband."

"Well clearly I was not very good at that when even with a promise from you to do absolutely anything I ask, you still will not marry me. Just as well I filled my time learning about Gothic romance novels and salacious books that the government has banned."

"Touché, my lady. So, have you read it?"

"Alas, no. If my father had a copy, it is not in his library and is well hidden. And while the young ladies at the finishing school knew of it, none were able to acquire a copy. Have you read it?"

For the first time ever, Lord Stephen Charville's colour heightened slightly. "I have."

"Do you have a copy?"

"I do."

"May I read it?"

"No. Not until after you are a married woman and are no longer an innocent."

Was he suggesting that he was willing to marry her? As she searched his face to understand his meaning, she realised his gaze was on her breasts. It moved slowly up to her lips, before eventually coming to rest on her eyes. They were heavy-lidded with passion now and she drew in a slow breath as he leaned forward, pressing his lips against hers.

Both his hands speared into her hair, tied loosely in a braid which hung down her back. He pressed her back onto the pillow.

As she parted her lips to allow him to slip his tongue into her mouth, he groaned in frustration, lifting himself onto his feet, without separating their lips. He kissed her for a few more moments, his tongue lazily sweeping her mouth then rasping against her tongue. He slowly withdrew, placing a final peck on her lips. As he stood straight, he caught her hands in his and placed a kiss on each set of knuckles.

"I shall sneak back in after the garden party to tell you how it went. I shall miss you. Remember to wash your hands after using the balm."

He executed a quick bow and was gone in a few seconds.

Harriet lay for a few moments just watching the door. What had he meant about letting her read Fanny Hill once she was married? Did he intend to marry her? Surely it would not be his place to give someone else's wife a profane book to read. Oh the man was such a puzzle to her. If she thought about it too much she would end up with a headache as well as a bellyache.

She opened the jar of salve, pulled down the covers and tugged up her nightrail. She may as well give it a try.

****

"Charville, not seen much of you this week. Where the devil have you been?" Stephen looked up from his conversation with the elderly Lady Bovington-Smythe to Lord Adam Cavanaugh and smiled genially at him.

"Cavanaugh, I have been busy showing the Earl of Oldbeck around. He has been out of society and I promised his sister I would look after him." Stephen nodded at William who was standing talking to the Dowager Duchess of Halimead, the current duchess and Mary. A loud laugh echoed around the area and Stephen's relatives smiled indulgently. He loved his family. They really did not bow to society pressures and had accepted Harriet's brother and sister-in-law to-be readily.

"Yes, I had heard. I am also hearing gossip about you

and Oldbeck's sister. Really, Charville? Harriet Weatherby?"

Stephen bristled.

"That's *Lady* Harriet to you."

"And what if imbecility runs in the family? Is that what you want for your heir?" The man nodded in William's direction.

"While your poor sister may be a pleasant enough young lady, she does have one thing that does not recommend her to me as a marriage partner. You. I would fear that my heir would be born with your bucked teeth, sticking out ears and disagreeable nature. Now while I believe the Earl of Oldbeck's condition does not run in the family, I would much prefer to take the chance that my son or daughter be agreeable and charming like the earl than resemble you in any way, my lord. Now, I do believe my sister-in-marriage is trying to catch my attention. I must attend her. Good day to you, Cavanaugh."

He bowed curtly and moved in Elizabeth's direction. Smiling politely at the Dowager Countess of Hempstile as he passed.

"Stephen, darling."

"Oh God, Lizzie, I think I have all but announced my betrothal to Lady Harriet Weatherby," he ground out.

"Well, given that your names were linked in the scandal sheets, I suppose it was only a matter of time before it was the honourable thing for you to do, brother-in-law, dearest."

"Poppycock, Lizzie. And tell me, why are you not in the country?"

Lizzie looked around her to check no one could overhear then she opened her fan and spoke very quietly.

"There was bleeding."

"Bleeding."

"Oh Christ, Stephen, you were a married man."

"Yes, yes, I understand. What does that mean? Are you still…?"

"I am. The physician said that some ladies bleed throughout. There is no rhyme or reason to it. But it could mean that I am losing the baby. Theo wants me to remain abed, but you know me."

"Yes, I do," he muttered. Why did women always refuse to follow their husband's instructions? Always seemed to think they knew better. "Just be careful, Lizzie. Anyway, what am I going to do about Harriet?"

"Well since you seem to be on given name terms with her, I'd marry the chit if I were you. Especially since you seem to have been kissing her quite thoroughly in the garden the other ni… Oh dear, what is wrong with William?"

He heard it then—William's voice raised and angry.

"Take it back, you s—s—scoundrel."

Stephen turned to see Cavanaugh standing grinning at William, Mary pleading with William, her hand on his arm, trying to pull him back. William wrenched his arm free from his fiancée.

"Oh come now, Oldbeck, I meant no harm. She is clearly not of our class. I just assumed she was a courtesan. A lovely courtesan, I grant you."

"She is no whore. Sh- she is g-g-oing to be my wife."

Fans wafted all around him as Stephen hurried over to the scene as gasps of horror were shushed so that the unfolding drama could be heard.

"What's wrong, Oldbeck? Can't bear for the babe in your kitchen maid's belly to be born a bastard? Come on, old man. She's been running off to the necessary every twenty minutes. She is obviously with child. Oh god, it is yours, is it not?"

Stephen reached him just in time to catch his coat sleeve and pull the punch wide, allowing Cavanaugh to dodge the fist. He threw his other arm around Oldbeck's waist and pulled him away, dragging him towards the house.

"No!" hollered William. They reached Elizabeth.

"Take Lord Oldbeck to your mother's morning room. I'll take Miss Callahan to Her Grace's bedchamber. Call me when he's calmed down," Elizabeth directed.

"Very well."

"I want satisfaction," cried William.

"I want a quiet life, Oldbeck. It seems we are both to be disappointed," Stephen grumbled.

When they reached the calm, blue-decorated morning room, William began to pace around the room.

"He said Mary was a whore."

"He did," said Stephen calmly, taking a seat on a high-backed chair and watching the younger man, ready to respond if he got too agitated.

"I cannot have that, Charville. A man has to look after his lady."

"I agree, Oldbeck. But a garden party is not a place to be throwing punches. It is the *only* reason I intervened."

"It is?"

"It is."

"Hmph!" He began pacing again having stopped to glare at Stephen. "It is just not acceptable, Charville. I should challenge him to a duel."

"Oldbeck, have you ever shot a pistol?"

"No."

"Have you ever fenced?"

"No."

"Have you ever had a lesson on how to box?" Oldbeck was now beginning to look like a surly youth.

"It is not my fault my father refused to send me to Eton."

"No, it is not, but you are ill-prepared for a duel. Besides, they are illegal. It would be bad enough for anyone else to go to prison but I doubt you would cope."

"I want ret… retr… repribrution."

"Retribution, you mean." Stephen sighed heavily and studied Oldbeck. Cavanaugh had been out of order. But what to do? "Let me think on it. Perhaps we can come up with something that will not get you thrown in prison but will get you some measure of satisfaction and a feeling that you have fought for your lady's honour."

Oldbeck sat down in a seat opposite Stephen, grinning. "You think you can? What will you come up with? Tell me, Charville. What could we do? I want Mary to be proud of me and to know me to be her champion. That Cavanaugh chap told everyone about the baby."

"Yes, I know. That is another problem. I think tomorrow you and I shall be paying a visit to the Archbishop of Canterbury."

"For a marriage licence?"

"For two marriage licences."

"But I only need one."

"Yes, you do. But I need one to marry Harriet."

"You are going to marry Harry?"

"Yes, and stop calling her Harry."

"Oh I must tell everyone."

"No, Oldbeck. I have not even told Harriet yet."

"How do you know she'll say yes?"

"Oh, she will."

"Oh, all right. Can we go and get Mary?"

"Yes. Let us go and get Mary then we shall collect Phoebe and then go home to Harriet."

****

"Ah, Mrs Aitken, just the person." Stephen had stopped the housekeeper just outside Harriet's room. He pulled her aside and began to speak in a low voice. "I must speak to Lady Harriet. You see I am going to accept her proposal of marriage. It cannot wait. Things have happened which mean it is imperative that Lord Oldbeck and Miss Callahan marry as soon as possible and we may as well arrange a double wedding. I appreciate it is not proper, and I promise not to do anything untoward. But we must speak privately on a number of matters. I am going to enter Lady Harriet's bedchamber now."

"My lord…"

He raised a hand to still her protest. "I know, Mrs Aitken. It is most improper. Thank the good Lord I am not Roman Catholic or I would be on my knees for a month for this transgression. But it is imperative. I would beg you to do your utmost to ensure as few servants as possible are aware of this visit. I would not want Lady Harriet's reputation ruined. Of course, within the week she will be a married lady so no permanent damage will be done anyway. I do not know how long our talk will take."

Mrs Aitken scowled and Stephen gave her his most charming smile. He could feel the ice beginning to melt. Before she had time to consider further, he slipped into the bedchamber and locked the door.

Harriet blinked and sat up, laying Northanger Abbey to the side, before straightening the bedcovers.

"Stephen, Mrs Aitken will be here any moment."

"Mrs Aitken knows I am here. I got her permission… well I left her with little alternative but she will make sure your reputation is safe. Oh God, Harriet, this afternoon was a disaster." He sat on the edge of the bed and removed his boots, then his coat.

"What are you doing?" she whispered.

He moved around the bed, placed Northanger Abbey on her lap and climbed on top of the counterpane and sat beside her.

"Getting comfortable. No one will disturb us. We need to talk and talk properly."

"Stephen, you cannot just come in here, half undress and sit on my bed."

"The door is locked and…" He moved onto one hip so he could look into her eyes. "If the offer of marriage is still available, I would very much like to become your husband, Lady Harriet."

She made a little gasp before drawing back slightly and focussing on him again. "You would?"

"I would. Yes. Have you changed your mind, Harriet?"

"No."

"Good, because something happened today but before I tell you about it, I want a betrothal kiss."

They kissed sweetly for a few moments and then he withdrew. He shuffled to lie on his side with his head on the pillow and she mirrored him. They gazed into each other's eyes and in that moment, Stephen knew that marrying Harriet was the right course for his life.

"There was a problem with William at the garden party. A gentleman taunted him and William became overset. The gentleman cast aspersions on Mary, suggesting she was a courtesan. William swung for him but not before the man had said loudly that Mary was with child."

"I see. Did William hurt the man?"

"No, I got there in time to grab his arm."

"May I ask who the gentleman was?"

"Lord Adam Cavanaugh."

"Oh!" Harriet crinkled her nose in disdain. "That does not surprise me."

"You know him."

"I do. Our fathers were close. They had a business deal that went wrong. They both blamed each other. When I had my first season the Cavanaughs decided it would be a fair way to make things right if I were to marry Adam. I was not keen but I gave him a chance. He was not a nice person. He was cruel about William and I told him I would not marry him. Then one night we were at Vauxhall Gardens. There was a large group of us. Somehow we were parted from the rest of the group and he drew me down one of those unlit paths. I tried to get him to take me back to our group but he refused. He pushed me up against a tree and tried to kiss me. I slapped him on the face. When that did not halt his progress, I hitched up my gown and used my knee to hit him between the legs. You see, it is not just William who used to take lessons from the stable hands. They used to teach me how to take care of myself. 'Lady 'Arriet' they used to say, ''Tis not safe for a young Lady ter be unable ter defend 'erslef.'"

Stephen guffawed with laughter at Harriet's common accent and the idea of her kneeing Adam Cavanaugh in the bollocks.

"Oh Harriet, you poor thing. What you must have gone through," he said trying to sound sober. The poor dear.

"Poor thing, my eye. Nothing poor about me, Stephen. I was unharmed. He only kissed me. And most of that was just his lips slobbering over my cheek like an overenthusiastic Labrador."

"Hmm, so he does not like your family then. Which is why he went for William. But William wants some kind of satisfaction for Mary. But he cannot duel. Has he any talents we could suggest?"

"He can ride. He is actually a very good and fast rider, if a little incautious on occasion. And Adam," her lips curved in a wicked smile, "is not really the best horseman in the world. There were not many things that my brother was good at growing up, but riding was one of them. He seemed to have a natural ability. My father said he was slow to learn to walk but as soon as he put him in a saddle on an old pony, he was off and did not look back. I always make a groom go with him because, as I said he can be incautious and would take jumps of which no rider or horse would be capable of taking. He gets over-excited. But in this instance his over-excitement may be useful."

"Interesting. Then I shall go to White's tomorrow and suggest a race down Rotten Row at dawn two days from now—after Oldbeck and I have been to see the Archbishop of Canterbury."

"What if he hurts himself?"

"You said yourself that Oldbeck is a good horseman, but I shall station friends along the route to help him if he falls. No doubt Cavanaugh will do likewise."

"Of course, you are right. I cannot help worrying for him."

"It is natural. But from now on you have me to help. We can worry together and find solutions together. I must admit that I do not know much about running an estate, but perhaps we could have a house party and I could invite my brother and he could go over the basics with us. Would that be acceptable? I do not want you thinking I am trying to take over but it was why you wanted me to marry you."

Harriet smiled.

"You know more than I do about running an estate. You had a better education than I did. I am afraid that embroidery and playing the pianoforte does not prepare one for deciding what crop rotation is necessary on one's estate. I shall be happy to leave it in your capable hands and for you to guide William. I am sure if I had wanted to, I could have learned the information needed but, I really did not want to. And with William behaving the way he was, I really just wanted a strong male role model for him."

"And I suited?"

"You are very strong," she said, her gaze roaming down his biceps and down to his waist. As it moved back up to his chest she licked her lips. "And very male."

"Oh, Harriet, you are such a tease. If you did not have a *headache*, I would be ripping off that nightrail and pre-empting our wedding vows. You really should not look at a gentleman in such a manner if you do not want him to ravish you."

She glanced back up at him. "Really? But I was just… admiring. You are very handsome."

And very hard, thanks to the way she was staring at him. Yes, climbing onto the bed with her had been a foolish idea.

"I should probably go," he said gruffly.

"Yes, though I wanted to talk to you about Phoebe."

"Phoebe?"

Well, talk of one's children was always a good way of dampening a man's ardour.

"Yes. You said you did not know what she needed and you knew nothing of gowns and bonnets and such. You are aware she is only six, are you not?"

"Yes. Of course I am."

"Well, children are children. She would probably be happy if you took her fishing. I know I was. When I was that age my father took both William and me fishing. William found it more difficult but he was the son and so my father had expectations. I think Papa was a little frustrated with William at times so it was handy having me along because he had success with me. Thus it was easier for him to be patient with William."

"So do things I would do with a son?"

"To an extent, yes. Do not dress her in breeches or cut her hair short but when in the country you can do things that are less ladylike. Of course she still has to learn the skills of a lady and now you are marrying me, I can undertake those tasks along with her governess. But you can teach her to play chess, teach her to ride—side saddle of course, skim stones across the lake and many other things you would do with a son. She is not a different species, Stephen."

He considered her words for a moment then nodded slowly. She was correct, most likely. And she had been a girl.

"I want to stay here all evening and just talk but I have been here too long already. Mrs Aitken will be having a fit of the vapours thinking I have debauched you."

"Stephen?" Harriet glanced down at her hands and inspected her nails. "On our wedding night, how shall I know what to do? I mean when you debauch me."

Oh God, she had no women in her family to ask. Mary probably would not be much help and no matter how close she was to Mrs Aitken, one just did not ask the servants. He lifted her chin, and gazed into her shining eyes. Without thinking on it, he pulled her into a tight hug, burying his face in her shoulder.

"Firstly, you will not be debauched. That is not a term that is appropriate for what will happen between us. We care for each other. We shall be making love. It shall be tender and sweet and perfect. And secondly, I shall send Elizabeth around the day after tomorrow. She shall take you and Mary shopping for your trousseaus and you can ask her any questions you like. Elizabeth is forthright. She will not beat around the bush. She will tell you exactly how things will be."

"Thank you."

He pressed a kiss to her temple then withdrew from her arms and lifted himself from the bed.

"Please do not take my lack of wanting to kiss you further as rejection, Harriet. If I were to start kissing you, I fear I would never stop."

"I understand. You smell delicious. Good enough to eat."

"You can eat me on our wedding night. I shall even show you how." He wiggled an eyebrow suggestively and she giggled. Stephen pulled on his boots and coat hastily, dropped a kiss on her head and removed himself from the room before his self-control waned. How had she worked her way under his skin so quickly?

But he knew how. Because she was sunshine in a Harriet-shaped package. And she had chased away the clouds allowing him to see life again as it should be experienced.

Chapter Eleven

Two mornings later, as the pink fingers of dawn snaked their way through the trees at Hyde Park Corner, Harriet shrugged deeper into her warmest pelisse and rubbed her hands together. There were a few ladies present but the vast majority of the crowd who had gathered to see the race between the Earl of Oldbeck and Lord Adam Cavanaugh were gentlemen.

William was up on his horse. Harriet eyed the gelding warily. Obviously it was not William's usual mount that was stabled in Oldbeck estate. But the Duke of Halimead had loaned him this animal, promising that it was fast but steady. Stephen and William had been in Hyde Park late yesterday afternoon trying him out and her brother had told her he was almost as good as Jim, his own horse.

Cavanaugh, on the other hand, looked out of sorts. Not many gentlemen of the *ton* enjoyed early mornings when in town and Harriet wondered if he had even been to bed yet. Was he even sober? She hoped the fellow did not have an accident. Partly because he may cause William to have one or hurt his own mount and partly because they would all feel responsible having suggested this race.

"Oh Lady Harriet, doesn't the earl look so handsome and strong?" said Mary, her cheeks pink with pride and something else that Harriet did not want to consider.

"Yes, he does," she said, a little non-committedly. She had never really considered her brother handsome but then she suspected no one ever thought much about the physical attributes of their siblings. She glanced over at Stephen. As William's number two, the lord sat astride a black gelding, also from his brother's stables.

It was a beautiful beast but Harriet suspected the animal's beauty came partly from the man sitting astride it. The muscles of his thigh flexed as he turned the horse in a wide circle. His motion was fluid, barely moving the reins, his crop resting against his shining top boot. His back was straight but relaxed as he gently touched his knee to the horse to bring it to a stop alongside William. He spoke in low tones to her brother, who smiled broadly and laughed loudly. Stephen clapped him on the shoulder and turned his horse towards them, finding Harriet in the crowd and giving her a warm, reassuring smile.

It was then that Harriet heard a discussion between two gentlemen who were just arriving.

"I put a hundred pounds on Oldbeck," said a tall young fellow.

"A hundred pounds on an imbecile. Are you addled in the brain too?" said the older gentleman who seemed to be a bit of a dandy if Harriet was any judge of gentlemen's clothing.

"I know a good bet when I see one. Look at the way he's sitting atop that horse. He knows his way around the beasts. Cavanaugh could not ride a donkey at a county fair."

"Possibly but Oldbeck is still an imbecile."

"Aye and I had a cousin who was called an imbecile. And he could out run all of us as children. I bet he could have as adults too if we had tried. Sadly my aunt put him in Bedlam and he was killed by another inmate. You have to hand it to the old earl that he never put that young man in one of these places. I hope he does well for himself. I wish him all the best. And it's good to see Charville being brought out of himself too. I hear he is to marry Oldbeck's sister. That could be a good match. So that's why my money is on Oldbeck. Charville does not back losers. He may be a second son but I'd wager he is as rich as Croesus."

Harriet listened in silence. It was nice to hear positive things said about William and her father's choice not to send William to an institution. It was even nicer to hear good things about her betrothed. It had never occurred to her that Stephen may be particularly rich. He certainly did not live an opulent lifestyle.

No matter. It was none of her business.

"Gentlemen, please move your horses to stand in line with me," called out a well-dressed gentleman." Harriet watched as William and Cavanaugh rode to their assigned places. Stephen and another gentleman on a horse—presumably Cavanaugh's number two—moved back. "I will say 'one, two, three, go.' When I say 'go,' you will start to ride to the end of Rotten Row where Lord John Windemere will be standing waving a red cloth. Turn your horses and ride back. The first person to pass me on horseback will be declared the winner. There is to be no pushing, no dirty tricks. I expect you both to behave like gentlemen. Understood?"

"Yes, I understand," shouted out William grinning. Cavanaugh nodded then lifted his head and looked at William, a sneer marring his features. A low chuckle went around some of the crowd. Harriet felt tears prick at the back of her eyes. Some of the men were making fun of her brother.

Mary squeezed her arm. Why was it the ex-maid who was no cleverer than her brother understood what these men—for one could not call them gentlemen—could not?

"Ignore them, Lady Harriet," muttered one gentleman who stood close by. "Your brother is a good man and a gentleman to boot."

She turned to the old man with white hair, piercing blue eyes and a kind smile.

"Thank you."

"No need to thank me. Just keep doing what you are doing. One day people like Oldbeck will be accepted in society more easily with young ladies like you championing their cause."

"Uncle James." Stephen approached on foot, sticking out his hand to shake the old man's hand.

"Stephen, my boy. I hear you are betrothed to this young lady. I read it in the morning paper. Congratulations. You are a lucky devil."

"Yes, I am."

"Stephen, get out the way," Harriet complained.

The man starting the race was counting down. Stephen jumped smartly out of the way, then squeezed in behind Harriet and Mary so he could watch the race from behind them.

Harriet leaned over the railing between Rotten Row and South Carriage Drive to see a plume of dust, two black coats, two horses' backsides and some hooves thundering away. Then she saw a gentleman's hat tumble off to the side.

"Oh well, that will be William's hat. He never could keep a hat on his head. Papa always said he must have an odd-shaped head."

"I shall go and get it," offered Mary.

"No, Mary, it is too dangerous. We can get it at the end and if not, well, it is only a hat." She turned to Stephen. "How long before they come back?"

"Rotten Row is less than a mile long. But with the turn, I think about five minutes at most."

"I should have been down at the other end. The turn is the dangerous part," Harriet mused.

"I have friends stationed all the way down the route, and Theo is at the end along with a surgeon friend of mine, just in case."

"Oh. You thought of everything."

"Well not everything. I did not think to tell William not to be so enthusiastic on the start line. I am sorry."

"Oh Stephen, that is William. People have to take him as he is or not at all. It upset me when everyone laughed but I should not let it bother me."

"Not everyone laughed," said the old man whom Stephen had greeted as Uncle James.

"No, I suppose not."

"Sorry, I never introduced you. Lady Harriet Weatherby, this Lord James Featheridge, my mother's uncle on her mother's side."

"It is a pleasure to meet you. May I introduce Miss Mary Callahan who shall soon be the Countess of Oldbeck?"

"It is a pleasure to meet you, Miss Callahan. I saw the announcement of your betrothal in the paper too."

Harriet smiled at the blush that crept up Mary's cheeks as the elderly gentleman bowed to her.

"Oh, I am going to be a countess. How grand." It seemed as if the thought had only just occurred to the maid. How odd that ladies in high society thought of nothing but the title they would gain through their marriage and yet Mary, who would gain such a lofty title from such a lowly estate had not even considered it. All she cared about was that she loved William.

"Yes, you are."

"Quick, they're coming back." Stephen was leaning past Harriet to see over the railing. "Excuse me." He pushed past Harriet, lightly squeezing her waist in a manner that no one else would have seen but that seemed slightly scandalous, then he bounded over the railing. Harriet and Mary pressed themselves against the wrought iron but all that could be seen was two dots and a plume of dust in the distance, obscured by the rays of the rising sun. Harriet adjusted the brim of her bonnet but it made no real distance.

"Who is in the lead?" asked Mary.

"I cannot tell from this distance," said Harriet."

"I fear it is the rider on the left," said Lord James.

"That would be Lord Cavanaugh."

"Aye it would."

"Come on William." Mary's piercing yell silenced everyone in the park. Harriet held her breath as all eyes turned to her but Mary paid them no heed. "Come on my darling, William. You can do it."

"Come on Oldbeck," joined in Lord James.

"Go for it Oldbeck!" came another voice.

"Get a move on Cavanaugh," a dissenting voice shouted.

"William, move!" screamed Mary.

Harriet stood and laughed as she watched the riders come nearer. Cavanaugh was in the lead but not by much. At last she could tell them apart. William, hatless and red-headed and definitely on the right.

"Come on, William," she muttered. "Please."

By now the shouting crowd were making a raucous noise and Mary was yelling at the top of her lungs. Harriet watched as William dug his heels hard into his mount, bending low, urging it to move faster. The horses were now neck and neck.

"This is for Mary," William cried out suddenly. This time there was no chuckling. It was as if everyone in Hyde Park stopped breathing. William's horse nudged ahead by about an inch, then two. They were approaching the gentleman who had started it. Cavanaugh grabbed at William's coat.

"No!" the ladies cried in unison.

But William was properly seated on his gelding, something that Cavanaugh was not. The other man began to topple, still holding on to William's coat. William attempted to shake him off. The finish was only a few strides away for the horses. Cavanaugh's horse closed the distance.

White material appeared at William's shoulder. His coat was ripping. A grunt from William as he shook ferociously and dug his heels into his horse. From where she was standing it was impossible to see which horse crossed the finish line first.

"Oldbeck wins," cried the gentleman who started the race.

"I beg to differ," shouted Cavanaugh's number two.

"Oldbeck crossed first. Be grateful I did not disqualify your man for ungentlemanly behaviour. Honestly, what a show, grabbing onto Oldbeck's coat like that. What a disgrace."

Gentlemen were jumping over the railings and surrounding the horses of William and Stephen—who had remounted his black gelding. Mary moved to go over but Harriet caught her arm and guided her away.

"Come, Mary. We shall see William and Stephen when they return home."

"But I wanted to congratulate William. He will be expecting me."

"No. This is his time to be with the gentlemen and accept praise and adulation and do male things. No doubt he shall have breakfast at his club. We shall have breakfast at home."

She looked at the crowd of men and caught Stephen's gaze. He held it for a few moments then she nodded.

"William is looking for you. Oh he sees you. Look at him and smile. That's it." William was grinning stupidly at his betrothed and she was grinning back. "Now hold his gaze for just a moment or two, then nod demurely and turn and come away with me." She did as she was told. Harriet caught her brother's gaze after Mary, nodded and winked then guided her charge out of Hyde Park and home for a verbal rerun of the morning's events.

Chapter Twelve

It had been a good day so far. William had won the race—though only just. Then he'd had breakfast in White's with Charville and his friends, who were now *his* friends it seemed. When he had got home, he'd sneaked upstairs with Mary and into his bedchamber. They had hugged and kissed and he'd tugged at her gown. He'd wanted to tup her but Mary kept saying if she was going to be a countess he could not tup her any more in the middle of the day. She had used her mouth on him till he had spilled his seed. She said he deserved it for winning the race for her honour. That had been very fine indeed. He had offered to do the same for her if she pulled her gown up but she'd said no. He didn't really understand what was going on with her except she had said she wanted to wait now until they were married.

The day before they had been to see the stuffy old Archbishop of Canterbury. He had hummed and hawed and suggested that William did not know his own mind. Stephen had been very calm but William could tell he was angry inside. Once he had said about the baby, the Archbishop had looked disapproving but had decided to give them the special licence, muttering something about not being responsible for another bastard on his watch.

Now Mary and Harriet were out shopping. William had just gone to the necessary and was re-joining Stephen and Whittingham in Stephen's library for brandy.

"To be honest, Whittingham, I shall be glad when William and Mary are married. I cannot bear another sodding week of trying to keep them apart. They were at it this morning as soon as our backs were turned. Oh I know the horse has bolted as far as any babes are concerned but it's what it looks like. Hopefully a few weeks of marital bliss and they get all the bed sports out of the way. Poor Mary will be walking as if she's ridden astride from John O'Groats to Land's End a couple of times and William's lust will have been slaked. The sooner the better for my money."

"Oh you poor devil. It must be a trial, especially with the delectable Lady Harriet so close."

"Watch what you say about Harriet, Whittingham. She is my intended and I shall have no salacious suggestions about her from you."

"Come now, Charville. You know what I meant. It must be difficult to know he is getting exactly what you want. That is all I was suggesting."

"Ah yes. Lucky beggar."

So Stephen wanted the wedding over and done with as quickly as possible. Well it could be done straight away. He had the special licence. He just needed Mary. He would go to Scotland. Everyone went to Scotland to get married, did they not? It could not be too far away. They'd be there by nightfall. Once Mary got home they would go to a coaching inn in London and hire a coach and driver… and horses of course. That would solve the problem. Then Stephen and Harriet would not have to worry. It was a perfect plan.

He turned from the library and made his way upstairs. They would have to stay a night in an inn. He would need to pack a bag. Then he would go to Oldbeck house and collect Mary for their great wedding adventure.

****

"Are you sure about this," Harriet said as she held the flimsy transparent nightrail up to her shoulders and allowed it to hang down as she inspected it. She turned towards the Duchess of Halimead, who, having insisted Harriet call her Elizabeth, was sitting on the bed, brimming over with glee and clapping her hands.

"Oh yes, Harriet, he will love it. Any man would. And Stephen is such a virile specimen. And you are so curvy. He shall practically spill in his dressing gown. Not that we want that of course."

"Spill. Oh Elizabeth, you keep talking of things I do not really understand."

"Spilling his seed, from his member. His manhood?"

"Ah."

Elizabeth proceeded to sit Harriet down and explain in quite graphic detail some of the things that went on in the bedchamber between man and wife. Some things seemed a little too unbelievable or intimate for Harriet to fully comprehend but she was willing to keep an open mind.

****

"William, I think Scotland is farther away that you think," Mary said, her face screwed up with concern.

"You do?"

"Yes."

"Maybe it will take a full day to get there?" He didn't want to put her or the babe at risk.

"Perhaps, I don't know."

"All right. We shall leave at dawn."

"William, are you sure that is what Lord Stephen meant?"

"I want to surprise him, Mary. I want him to see that we won't be a burden to him."

"I know. Once we are back at Oldbeck estate we can show him properly."

"Yes. Now lift you skirts so I can do for you what you

did for me this morning."

"No, not until we are married."

God, he wanted her so much. He was hard as a rock. Why was she being so difficult? But he knew no means no and if a woman says no then you do not press her or force your attentions on her. These were the rules. Just like you do not hit girls, you don't show your cock in public and you don't talk about pissing or shitting in public—oh yes and the new rule of not talking about tupping in public. He had to keep reminding himself of that.

"Mary, do you think you will ever want to do it again?"

"Yes. I do want to do it. Nearly all the time. Especially when we are together. But I'm trying to be a lady and ladies do not do it before they are married."

"I do not see the difference now the babe is on the way, but have it your way. But you need to be ready to leave at dawn. We shall walk to the coaching inn and hire a coach from there. I shall have the marriage licence and a valise of my clothes. Will you be all right to carry a valise with your clothes downstairs?" He stared at her belly which did not seem round yet. He wondered when it would get round. He had been told that ladies had to be careful about carrying heavy weights and over-exerting themselves when they were increasing.

"Of course, William. Please do not fuss."

"I shall of course carry your valise to the coaching inn, for I am a gentleman. But you cannot let the servants know. They would tell Harriet and she would cause a fuss. I do not think she would be pleased."

"Perhaps not."

"Well, she will just have to like it. I am sick of Harriet telling me what to do. I am the earl and her title is a… what is the word again…c…curtsey… no no, that's not it. But it's like that word. But you know what I mean. Stephen said I must act like an earl and from now on I am going to be in control. You must leave this letter on the desk before you leave in the morning."

"I will," Mary answered, placing a delicate peck onto his cheek. Sometimes it seemed she did not want to kiss him on the mouth for fear she would make him want more—which of course he would.

"Soon we shall be a family. You, me and our babe."

"And once we are married we shall even see each other without any clothes on whatsoever."

Heat rushed up his cheeks and into his breeches at the thought. She'd be like some of the paintings he had seen in the art galleries. He had probably seen every part of her at some point while tupping her but they had never, ever taken all their clothes off. It seemed almost sinful. Like Adam and Eve.

"I need to go." Why was his voice all squeaky? It was as if he was ill and was unable to speak because he had just had a coughing fit. Mary's cheeks looked very pink too. Was she imagining him without clothes too? Oh he had to go. He would have to hide in an alcove for a few minutes before going down the stairs to allow his cock to go down but he had done that on many an occasion since it had first seemed to gain a life of its own when his body changed from that of a child into that of a youth. "Be outside at dawn. I love you, Mary." He dared not touch her again. He left, found an alcove and breathed deeply until he would not get into trouble for upsetting the maids or his sister. Then he hurried down to convince Stephen to leave. He had packing to do.

****

Harriet scowled at her coddled eggs and toast, wondering where on earth Mary could be. Since Mary had been in service for years, it was usually she who was up with the lark, and Harriet who wandered in as Mary was finishing her last sip of tea. Had the girl taken ill in the night? Was there something wrong with the baby? Perhaps she should send a servant up to check on her.

Just at that moment the door opened. Unannounced by the harried butler whose head she could see just behind her betrothed and his daughter, Lord Stephen Charville stalked into the room. Phoebe seemed to be panting, her delicate brows furrowed and her pelisse buttoned up wrongly. The poor child did not even have on her bonnet. She was dragging it behind her like an unwanted toy.

"My lord, what…"

He looked around the room then speared her poor footman with a stare.

"Take Miss Phoebe to the nursery, make sure she is given breakfast and ask Miss Paton to begin her lessons for today whether Miss Callahan is in attendance or not. We shall ring for a servant when we require anything else."

"Yes, my lord."

The footman glanced at Harriet who nodded her assent at the boorish behaviour of her intended. Really it was rather beyond the pale for him to march in here, bypass her butler and start ordering her servants about. He then dismissed the butler with a nod.

When they were quite alone, he ensured the door was shut, then he turned the key in the lock.

"Good morning, Phoebe. How is my step-daughter-to-be this fine morning? I see your father forgot to dress you properly, you poor child," she said to the closed door, the sarcasm dripping off her tongue.

"Do not start this morning, Harriet. Your tongue is too sharp for a man who has not yet had a cup of tea or a slice of toast, far less a kiss from his favourite lady."

"My tongue is sharp because you barge into my house, order my servants around and lock my breakfast room door as if you are… going… to…"

"To what?"

He advanced, taking her hand and drawing her to her feet. Then he tilted her chin as one hand moved around her waist and settled on her bottom.

"Ravish me?" she said on a shaky breath.

He pressed a delicate kiss to the side of her neck as he pushed his long, fingers into her coiffure.

"Not today, my Harriet." He kissed again, lower this time. "Not that I would not want to."

"I would allow you to ravish me," she admitted with a little laugh, surprising even herself.

He kissed her collarbone then ran his tongue along the little indentation.

"I know. But we have only a few more days to wait. And then we can take our time and savour one another, slowly."

"It may sound silly but I wish we could do it now and get it over with."

"Why?" He lifted his head and gazed into her eyes, his darting about as he tried to discern the meaning behind her words.

"Elizabeth said it would hurt."

"The first time—a little. I hesitate to mention Sarah again. I do not wish you to think I compare you to her but she is the only virgin I have made love to. She said it hurt for only a minute or two. The first night we could not make love more than a couple of times to stop her getting sore but we found other ways to appreciate one another. You and I shall too."

"I do not mind you talking of Sarah. She was your wife and she was Phoebe's mother. She was as much a part of your life as I hope I shall be."

"Good, because while I still hold her in my heart, there is plenty of room for you both."

He pressed his lips to her neck again, moving them up towards her ear.

"Stephen, is it... is it hard just now?"

"Mmnh? Is what hard just now?" He bit down on her earlobe as he moved one hand to cup her breast. Just as he was starting to pepper light pecks along her jaw he stopped. "Oh that! God, Harriet, you are the most vexing yet delightful creature I know. Why do you ask?"

"I want to touch it."

"Oh you do. Well for your information, my lady, it is getting there and no, you are not touching it."

"Oh." Well that was rather disappointing. Elizabeth had said that when a man started kissing and fondling a woman, his member became hard and Stephen's was merely getting there. Perhaps it was memories of Sarah that was causing the issue. Elizabeth had said that being upset or worried could cause a problem and not to nag him about it. "Well, not to worry. We really should…"

"Not to worry about what, Harriet?" He lifted her chin and caused her to make eye contact with him but his eyes gleamed with merriment and a smile tugged the corners of that delicious mouth.

"Nothing," she said, as brightly as she was able.

"What else did Lizzie say?"

"Oh, lots of things."

"I suspect your education on the male anatomy is incomplete." He leaned down to whisper in her ear. As his breath brushed across the small hairs, she shivered slightly. "Worry not, Harriet, my love. When I was imagining you in my arms last night and I was unable to sleep, everything down there was in perfect working order. Today however I am concerned that your brother sneaked out of my house either in the night or at dawn and is currently warming your charge's bed. My daughter is in your nursery and the servants shall be wondering what exactly we are doing in here. All these things make it difficult for a man to fully concentrate on what a beautiful and sensual woman he has in his arms."

He captured her lips this time, sliding them slowly across hers, using his tongue to probe for access to her mouth. She opened to him, welcoming the invasion of his tongue and the clash of his teeth against hers. She pushed her hands into his curls and allowed him to carry her away on the bliss of the togetherness they found whenever they let their lips meet. All too soon he was pulling away.

She leaned against him, catching her own breath, wondering at what point since she had met Lord Stephen Charville had the perfectly competent Lady Harriet Weatherby's brains turned to pudding? Why was it that when she saw him she became weak at the knees and unable to think about anything but his kisses and the feel of his strong hands on her back and in her hair? Perhaps she had been too harsh on William. Falling in love made one unable to think rationally and only able to react with one's body. No wonder he had sought out Mary at every opportunity.

Stephen pressed a kiss to the top of her head. "We have to stop," he said, his own breath slightly ragged. "If not, I shall ruin you." He moved his mouth back to her ear. "And yes, Harriet. It is hard—as stone and it is your doing, my beautiful innocent bride to be. Now, come let us go and sort out your brother and the other bride-to-be in this household."

****

William was beginning to feel a little uneasy. He had butterflies in his belly and it had nothing to do with Mary sitting beside him, her head on his shoulder as she dozed, her hand lying protectively over her tummy. He still could not see anything.

He had plenty of money but the driver they had hired had given him a couple of funny looks when he had said he had wanted to go to Scotland. The driver had said it would cost to change horses in coaching inns and tonight was not looking good for driving through the night. William had accepted they would have to spend tonight in an inn. So Scotland was two days away. What did it matter? They would still be married quicker than if they waited the week and Charville would still be pleased.

When the driver had said he was not sure, William had pulled out his purse and asked how much for the whole journey up front. That had made the difference. The driver had calculated it, William had managed to get the driver to reduce the amount by a few shillings and they had both been happy with the result and William and Mary still had plenty of coins for inns and horses and to pay the blacksmith at Gretna Green.

But now they were out of the hustle and bustle of the city, he was no longer so sure of himself. Yes, he was an earl and grown up. But he had never been truly on his own. He had Mary of course. But he understood enough to know that Mary was like him and neither he nor Mary was clever and people could take advantage of him. What if the driver had already taken advantage of him?

He looked at his betrothed and at her belly. A tear welled up under his lash and he swiped it away. Damned tears. Grown men didn't cry. But what if he could not look after them? What if he failed? He knew people in the *ton* thought he should be in some institution for imbeciles. What if he and Mary became too much for Harriet and Stephen when they had a family of their own? Stephen did not know but that was what Cavanaugh had said before he had insulted Mary at the garden party. And William had been too scared to talk to Stephen about it.

He pressed his nose against Mary's head, breathing in the smell of her freshly washed hair as his tears dripped onto it. He had to make this work. For Mary as much as for himself.

****

"Should we open the door?" Harriet asked as they stood outside Mary's bedchamber.

"Christ, Harriet, the time for being prim and proper is over." Stephen felt bad about his blasphemy but he was ready to wring William's neck. "Oldbeck, are you in there?" he hollered through the door.

Harriet raised both her eyebrows, her hands on her

hips as she glared at him. He had a feeling this was going to be the face he got whenever he was in trouble.

"Try the handle. Surely they would lock the door if they were doing anything untoward."

Stephen gave her a dubious look.

"He did impregnate her in a hayloft if you remember."

Harriet sighed. "Really, my lord. Do you have to be so... so..."

"Honest?"

"I was reaching for vulgar, but honest will do."

Stephen reached for the door handle and turned. He opened the door, his eyes half shut, dreading what he might see, but the bed was made and the room appeared to be empty.

A sigh behind him made him smile at his companion's innocence.

"My darling, there are other places than the bed to make love. Besides, if they are not here, then where?"

"Oh!"

"Quite."

He moved into the room, which was obviously completely empty. He checked behind the door of the dressing room—also empty. Though had they been there, he suspected he would have heard something. Having slept in a room near William for the better part of a week, Stephen knew that the earl snored like a coach and six crossing a wooden bridge at speed.

"Come, let's search the house."

It did not take long to search the townhouse with all the servants looking too. There were not many places that two adults could hide. When they reached the library, Harriet stared at the envelope on the desk. In a scrawled childish script was her name. She clutched at Stephen's wrist.

"Oh no, what has he done?"

"Now Harriet, do not panic until you have read it."

She picked up the letter opener and cracked the seal,

pulling out the sheet of vellum.

Dear Harriet and Stefen
I no you want Mary and I to be marryd as quiclie as possible. So we have ~~hyre~~ hired a coach and gone to Skotland. I no it will tayke a day or too to get theyre but it is still ~~qu~~ faster than waiting a weak. Stefen said he coold not wait for us to be wedd.
Pleese do not be angry. It will be a grate advenchure just like Robinsin Krooso.

Yours ~~afect~~ affektioniteltly
William, Earl of Oldbeck
Your brother
(I love you Harriet. And Stefen, please tayke good cayre of Harriet until we get home).

Harriet's hand covered her mouth and she sank against Stephen's body as the hand holding the letter trembled.

"It will be all right," he said, his mind whirring. How long had they been gone, how long would it take to catch up to them and convince them to return to London? Could he convince Harriet to stay here? Of course he couldn't. He would have a better chance of convincing the tide on the Thames not to come in.

"How will it be all right, Stephen? He thinks Scotland is a couple of day's journey away. He thinks Robinson Crusoe is a great adventure. In the last bit of the story that you read to him the idiotic young man had been captured by pirates."

"They cannot have much of a head start. I shall get Theo's best coach and team. William will have a hired coach and horses. They shall be a team of old nags ready for the knacker's yard. Theo is a snob when it comes to his cattle. We shall catch them in no time."

"Fine. You go to Halimead House and arrange for the coach. I shall send a servant to your house for a valise of clothes for you and get a maid to pack clothes for me. I shall arrange for a picnic hamper of food for us. What about Phoebe?"

"Miss Paton can take her round to Halimead house after her lessons. She can stay with Theo and Lizzie," said Stephen. He bent and pressed a quick kiss to her lips. "I should forbid you to go, but I suspect I would be wasting my breath."

"You would. Besides, Mary may need a woman there."

"Possibly, though I doubt she is in danger from William."

"No, but can he protect her properly?"

Stephen considered it, then nodded. "I think he would die trying. Come, let us make haste before that theory is put to the test."

****

"Guvnor!"

William looked around at the coach driver who was scratching his chin and looking a little concerned. "Yes."

"I don't mean to butt in nor nothing, but may I suggest that you ask the innkeeper for a private room for you and your lady to dine in. She seems like quite a finely dressed young lady and I don't believe the taproom is the place for her. She got some funny looks at lunchtime."

"Oh. A private room."

"Yeah. They'll have a few in here. It's a good inn. I use it regular, like. I also suggest you ask for adjoining rooms. You have no chaperone and no ring. May I suggest you use your surname and say you are Mister and Missus? Pretend to be married, like. I assume you're eloping since we're going to Scotland."

William smiled. This driver was very clever. He nodded.

"Oh we are. I love her very much. We were to marry in London but Scotland is quicker. I even have the special licence right here." He tapped his coat.

"You don't need a special licence in Scotland, Guvnor."

"Oh." Well the trip to see the grumpy old Archbishop had been a bit of a waste, had it not? Never mind. Stephen had got his special licence too.

But he would do as the driver had said. He would tell the innkeeper they were Mr and Mrs Weatherby and he would ask for a private room in which to dine. Harriet would be proud when he told her about it. Again that gnawing feeling came back. An uneasiness. He missed his sister already. She annoyed him when she told him what to do and nagged him not to use rude words in front of ladies, but she really was a good egg when all things were added up.

Chapter Thirteen

Harriet sat up straight as Stephen poked his head back in the carriage door. Even in the darkness she could see the shake of his head.

"They have not seen them, not that they are willing to say at least, but I believe them."

Harriet could feel the now familiar prickle of tears at the back of her eyes. Fear warred with the sense that William had been brought up well enough to be able to cope in most circumstances. And Mary should be wise enough, should she not?

"What now?" she asked, knowing the answer full well.

"There is no moon and it is beginning to drizzle. We cannot take a chance of hurting the horses or damaging the carriage. I will not put men or you in danger. William has money. He should have been able to afford a room at an inn."

"As long as he has not been set upon by highwaymen," she said.

"Aye, as long as that has not happened. Harriet, they only have one room left. I told them we shall take it. I told them we were Mr and Mrs Charville."

His hand was reaching for hers in the dark, fumbling for her acquiescence and for her to understand their predicament. She turned over her gloved hand, clasping her fingers around his.

"What do a few days matter? There is no one to see us

and even if there are, we have our special licence."

"I have no reputation with which to be concerned and as far as I am concerned, we shall be wed by this time next week. Therefore it is in your hands. I shall sleep in the servants' quarters if you say no, my love."

"I want you to share my room."

"As you wish."

As he helped her climb down from the carriage, a knot formed in her belly. Excitement and nervousness coiled into each other. Would he ruin her this evening? Was this the night she would become a proper woman with all the knowledge of which Elizabeth had talked. It had sounded so decadent and wonderful and intimate.

Stephen organised the bags and led her into the inn. By the time she saw this courtyard again, she would no longer be an innocent lady. She snuggled deeper into her pelisse and quickened her step.

****

"Is it not to your liking?" Stephen asked as Harriet pushed the beef around her plate absentmindedly. She was only vaguely aware that he had spoken.

"Sorry? Oh I apologise. I really am not particularly hungry."

He scowled at her plate and she looked at the food piled high. It really was not the nicest inn she had ever stayed in and the food was edible at best.

"I do not want you becoming ill, Harriet."

"No, I suppose you do not. That would never do," she said, moving some peas to join the piece of beef she had just moved. She was sure you could saddle a horse with the meat it was so tough.

Stephen stood and walked a few paces away from the small table in their bedchamber. He had arranged for supper to be brought to them because of the late hour and she really did appreciate it. But now she was tired and out of sorts and worried about William and Mary.

"They shall be fine," he said eventually.

"You do not know that."

"Harriet, if two imbeciles had been set upon by robbers on the Great North Road, you can bet your life that the story would have reached every inn from London to Gretna Green."

Harriet gasped. Stephen had never called William an imbecile, far less Mary. He had always been too much of a gentleman.

"Does William know you call him an imbecile behind his back?"

"No, because I do not. I never have. But that would be the story that would have carried far and wide. We would be aware of it. My love, you know that anyone who meets William knows that he is not, well, I do not need to spell it out. And Mary hardly comes across as a bluestocking. They may be easy pickings but they would also be easy to spot. Which would mean any ill that had befallen them would have quickly travelled. I apologise. Please do not be angry with me. I care for William and Mary and want to see them safe as much as you do."

And he did. Harriet knew that he did. The signs were obvious in the creases around his eyes and mouth and in the way he had barked instructions at the driver. And yes, even in the way he had just lost his temper with her.

She walked towards him and placed her arms around his waist. And Stephen enveloped her in his embrace.

"Are we going to make love now?" she asked, breathing in the spicy scent of him, as she moved her cheek over the silk of his waistcoat.

Stephen pulled away slightly and frowned down at her. "No, my love. We share a bed tonight because there is no choice and your reputation will be damaged if we are caught but I shall not take your innocence. Not until our wedding night."

"But you said this morning if I touched you, you

would… You talk of pre-empting our wedding vows. You suggest that you would like to… tup me."

"Those are just words borne of frustration. My body may want to but it is not right."

"You have had other women… since Sarah."

"Actually, no, I have not."

"I thought men always had mistresses and courtesans."

"Most do but not me."

"I see. Well… I do not see, but there my argument runs out. I can hardly be jealous when you have not had other women."

"I suppose not."

She moved away from him, walking towards the dressing table, pulling pins from her hair.

"And you are able to…"

"Yes."

"It is just that Elizabeth said…"

"Elizabeth says more than her prayers. Do you need a maid?"

"Not if you undo the buttons at the back of my gown and the laces of my stays. Can you do that?"

"You would not be the first lady I have undressed."

"I am not sure whether to be relieved or dismayed at that information."

Harriet was not sure that this was the kind of intimacy she wanted with Stephen. He was now trying to haul off one of his boots. She turned, grabbed the heel of the offending item and tugged. They were well made and snug. It took a few hard yanks until the boot began to slide off over his heel.

She adjusted her stance in time to stop herself from falling on her derriere. Then she wiggled her fingers to indicate he should lift his other foot. In another few minutes he was standing in his stocking feet slowly tweaking the buttons of her gown loose.

She held her breath as he pushed the fabric of her carriage gown off her shoulders. Then she stepped out of the garment and laid it over the chair. When she straightened, she was more aware of Stephen than she had been of him at any other time this day. His hot breath on her neck as he swept her hair forwards over her shoulder again, the slight scrape of a fingernail as he caught up the ribbon, the heat of his body, the smell of his shaving soap.

"It is knotted. Wait a moment. Ah there." Her stays loosened and Harriet hauled in a welcome breath as the small bones released her ribcage.

"Better?" he said, his fingers massaging her side, under her arms and round underneath her breasts.

"Much," she said, almost sinking back against him. Suddenly he crossed his hands in front of her, drawing her fully against him, then kissed her on the cheek.

"You are far too tempting, Lady Harriet Weatherby."

"Soon-to-be Lady Stephen Charville."

"But not yet."

"As near as makes no difference."

"It makes a difference to me."

"Should it not be me who is all missish about this?"

"I am not being missish. I am being a gentleman. Now go into that dressing room and get on your nightrail and I… bloody hell."

"What?"

"I do not even own a night shirt. I sleep in the nude."

"Well then, it looks as though I shall at least see your naked form before our wedding night." An ache settled between her legs at the mere thought. Was he muscular like the farm workers when they took off their shirts? Did he have hair on his chest?

"I shall wear my shirt. It is quite long enough."

And I shall wear my shift. I never travel with a nightrail. It is easier to get dressed if there is an emergency in the night if one is simply wearing a shift."

"Really?" The look of horror on his face made her laugh.

"It is practical. I thought men liked practical."

"We do. But tonight it is not practical."

She undid her petticoats and stepped out of them, turning to him and smiling.

"It looks as if we are both ready to retire then." She picked up a ribbon and tied her hair loosely at the nape of her neck, then walked over to the bed. "Is it all right if I take this side?" she asked hesitantly.

He moved to the other side, sat and waved a hand over his shoulder as he bent to remove his stocking. She climbed in and tried to look uninterested as he unbuttoned the fall of his breeches.

"Devil take it," he muttered as he straightened, scowling at the fire. He walked over to it and began to bank it for the night. Harriet's gaze roved up his strong, hair-covered calves, then his thighs, which she had so admired in breeches as they had caressed the sides of his horse only yesterday. His shirt covered his modesty but she wondered how far up the hairs travelled.

"Are you enjoying the view of my arse, my lady?" he grumbled as he set the fireguard in place.

Harriet pursed her lips, trying to look sombre and failing miserably. "I am sure I do not know what you mean, my lord. And I would appreciate if you would moderate your language in front of me."

"Really?" He walked around the room, snuffing out all the candles but the one at his side of the bed. "And this from the young lady who asked me to tup her in the library earlier this week. Tup is such a crude word, would you not agree? Was it not you who chastised your brother for using that very word when we first met?"

"That was different."

"In what way?"

"It just is. We were not in private then. And now I have finished with this conversation, my lord. Good night."

As she turned away from him to lie on her right side, she felt the other side of the mattress depress. Good lord, they were in bed together, like man and wife. Just his shirt and her shift separating their naked bodies. Why could she not breathe? She could not hold her breath all night.

When he placed his hand on her bare arm and pressed his wet lips to her shoulder, she let out her breath on a sigh.

"Do not go to sleep when you are vexed with me. For the most part I was teasing."

She rolled onto her back and into his arms.

"I am only slightly vexed with you. I am more vexed with myself for being foolish enough to think that you were interested in me over and above the honourable promise you made me when I saved Phoebe. That you can wait and you were only teasing about not being able to wait shows me how truly innocent and naïve I am. I really was foolish enough to believe that you burned with passion for me as it states in all those lurid novels that I read." She let out a little self-deprecating laugh.

"I suspect you should be more vexed with me than you are for I have not explained myself well. I was not teasing when I said I want you. I really do burn for you, Harriet, even if I would not quite put it like that. It is such an over-dramatic phrase. I was teasing when I said I would take you though. I will not allow myself to have you even though I want you very much and tonight, lying so close and not being able to make you mine in every sense of the word shall be pure torture."

"Then have me."

"No. Harriet, until I put that ring on your finger, you must have the option of changing your mind. If I ruin you, you have no option but to marry me."

"I shall not change my mind. It was I who asked you to marry me."

"It matters not. You are the one who cannot go back once the deed is done."

"You are a very stubborn man, Lord Stephen Charville."

"And you are a very stubborn woman. We shall have an interesting marriage."

He pressed his lips to hers and she opened immediately, eliciting a deep groan from the back of his throat as he moved slightly atop her. Stephen was in no hurry and the passion he exuded was leisurely as he massaged her lips slowly, dipping his tongue in and out of her mouth, tasting, tickling, licking, rubbing. Harriet moved her hands slowly up and down his spine, not daring to explore further, not wanting to remind him of his promise not to ruin her. If he did remember, he may stop kissing her.

One side of his muscled chest pressed against one of her soft breasts, his thigh against one of hers. Eventually he withdrew his mouth and smiled. His gaze was hooded with lust and he trailed the fingertips of one hand down her side, ticklish yet sensual.

"Just because I refuse to ruin you does not mean I cannot show you pleasure, my beautiful bride-to-be. I may be fit for Bedlam by the end of tonight but at least you will know the pinnacle of ecstasy."

"I do not quite understand…"

"Do you have another shift with you?"

"Yes. One for tomorrow. Why?" She gasped as he moved under the sheet and caught one of her nipples in his mouth through the thin cotton of her undergarment. In seconds the material was damp with his saliva. "Oh Stephen."

"Do you like that, my love?" he asked, moving to the other breast.

"Very much," she managed, raking her fingers through his hair. He sucked on the hard peak and she gasped as sensation ripped through her insides into the most private part of her, as though her breast and that part of her were joined on a string.

"Oh Harriet, you are a wonder to behold. You are so sensual." Stephen kissed along the side of her breast, flattening the cotton as he moved, tweaking her other nipple. Harriet was aware of a sort of tension and a need to move. She was restless under his touch but she did not want him to stop. Anything but that.

"Please, Stephen." She did not know for what she asked. For him to return to suckling on her nipple. He seemed to know instinctively what she needed because he bit gently on the hard nub and she hissed in surprise, but not pain, then the wet cotton was swirled to soothe.

Stephen moved his hand even while he continued to suck and lave at first one breast then the other. Harriet wondered if it was possible to go mad under an onslaught of such sensations. Slowly and carefully as if he was petting a horse that may spook, he caressed his fingers down her ribs, over the roundness of her belly, out to her side and over her hip. Then he drew them in to her feminine place, where the nest of red curls was covered by her shift.

"Open your thighs, love," he murmured gently. She did as she was bade. If she was going to marry him, this was not time to become shy. Biting her lip and closing her eyes, she parted her legs. "Look at me, Harriet. I promise, you shall like it."

Giving him a shy smile, she gathered her courage and opened her lids. His gentle smile melted her heart. Gone was the joking Stephen who had vexed her so badly earlier. He ran the back of his fingers over her curls and onto the intimate flesh underneath. It tickled, but something else too. She squirmed slightly. The second stroke of his hand was a slightly firmer touch, less tickle and more of the feeling that made her crave more of his touch. Her body instinctively moved towards it.

Stephen kissed up her chest and throat as he pressed his fingers into the intimate creases of her flesh, seemingly unhindered by the cotton between his fingers and her womanhood. Then he moved his middle finger backwards. She wriggled slightly, trying to discourage him. He had made her excited and somehow she knew she was damp there. He would feel it and she would be embarrassed, for she did not understand what caused that dampness. No one had ever quite explained it but she was sure it had something to do with her courses.

She wriggled again as he pressed the cotton into the dampness.

"Shh, Harriet. God, you're so wet for me." His voice was reverent. As though the wetness was a good thing. He caressed his hands and the material through her damp flesh, a groan escaping him. Then he lifted his hand and licked his fingers, smiling at her. "Like nectar," he whispered.

She was flabbergasted. There was no other way to describe it.

"Do you want me to stop?" he asked, concern creasing his brow.

She shook her head vehemently, unable to speak but sure of one thing—stopping was the last thing she wanted him to do.

He nodded solemnly and returned his fingers to her folds, moving them until he found one small area that made her writhe and mewl. She grasped his shoulders and rocked into his touch, lifting her mouth to his lips for a kiss. He covered her mouth with his, pushing his tongue immediately into her mouth and swirling it gracelessly and desperately around. It was as if he was trying to consume her. She was reminded of their first kiss—brutal and needy yet not frightening in the least. He tugged her against him and it was then that she felt the hardness of his manhood against her thigh.

Stephen moved one leg between hers and rubbed it up and down her leg, groaning into their kiss as he pressed his fingers more insistently upon her intimate spot. Then he began to move down, kissing her neck again, her chest and finally capturing her nipple between his lips. As he did so, his hardness rubbed deliciously against her thigh.

Harriet closed her eyes and pushed a hand through his

hair. It was absolutely divine to feel his lips on her breasts. And the hardness against her thigh filled her with anticipation, though she did wonder how something so large would fit inside her. This is what Lizzie had meant about men becoming lost in their own passions.

My, but he looked wonderful. So virile, with sweat glistening on his brow, his eyes dark with passion, his jaw set and determined as he let go of one breast and without lifting his head rooted for the other.

Suddenly he stopped.

"Devil take it. This is why I did not want to do this. I knew this is what would happen."

"What?"

"Nothing. Let me go and I shall sort myself out in the dressing room."

He moved to climb over her and get out of bed but Harriet was in no mood for it. She was innocent and confused and he could just explain to her what the devil was going on. She raised her knee and wrapped her arms around his neck, effective jamming him between her legs.

"What the devil…"

He moved.

It felt….

Well it felt wonderful. His hardness now rested against her most intimate place.

"Let me go, Harriet."

"Not until you explain why you were fine one minute then trying to escape the next."

"Because I nearly lost control. And devil take it but lying like this, I'm about to lose it again."

"Perhaps if you stopped wriggling, it would not feel so good."

"Harriet, I… let me go."

"Not until you explain."

"Fine… If you must know, the truth is that I do not want to make love to you until our wedding day because it has been such a long time since I have been with a woman that I fear I will lose control and it shall be... well... disappointing for you. I thought if I did not penetrate you that somehow I could control myself and you would see how good lovemaking could be and so the wedding night would not matter so much. But now..." he moved against her, long strokes of his hardness against her aching womanhood. She saw the moment he gave in. The moment the defiance left his gaze and passion resumed. She moaned and rolled her head on the pillow, digging her heels into the mattress. "Now I could not stop if I tried."

"Then do not stop, my love, because that feels wonderful."

"You are going to be the death of me, my lady," he murmured, moving down onto his forearms and pressing a kiss to her neck. "Wrap your legs around me, my darling, and tell me when it feels as if you might burst with the tension."

He pressed his mouth over hers again, kissing her passionately, ramping up her need for him. Their clothing was now rumpled and scrunched between them but still they did not touch skin to skin at the place where they rocked against one another.

He pushed his hands under her buttocks, pulling her ever harder against him. She pushed and rocked, reaching for that something that she could not yet describe—did not understand—yet somehow knew was the secret that married women held back from innocents.

Harriet pulled her mouth away from his, burrowing her head in his shoulder, concentrating on finding whatever her now slow, determined movements craved.

"Oh God. Oh Stephen, please... help me."

"Let go, my love," he crooned. "Let it happen."

Something snapped inside her and a cry escaped her lips as a wave of euphoria surged through her body. She clung to Stephen as if he was her lifeboat in a storm. He continued to stroke his hardness against her. She was trembling, her body awash with sensations and feelings she had never imagined possible. She gasped in breaths and Stephen nuzzled her neck gently.

"Well done, my Harriet," he murmured into her flesh. "You are beautiful when you come. Beautiful always but more beautiful when you come apart in my arms. I should stop now but I cannot. I pray you shall forgive my crudeness and ungentlemanly behaviour. I am too close to the edge, you see."

Then he wrapped his arms more tightly and began to thrust harder against her, apologising every dozen seconds or so. Harriet tightened her grip and kissed his neck. She did not want him to apologise for this. It was wonderful. And she had been warned he may become caught up in himself at the end. What was it he had said to her?

"Let go, my love," she whispered. She hoped he did not think she sounded like an imbecile. Perhaps only men said it to ladies. But his rhythm had faltered and he thrust a few more times.

"Oh Christ," he growled. His body stiffened and he made a feral grunting noise. She noticed the veins standing out on his neck. He thrust slowly a few more times. And then he stopped, propped up on his elbows over her, sweat dripping from his face, panting and dishevelled, a wary look in his eyes. He looked the most handsome she had ever seen him. She smiled reassuringly at him.

"Well, my lord, I am not sure whether I should accept your apology. If I accepted your apology, I fear that you would be unwilling to do this again. And I would very much like to do this again."

"At the end," he gasped. "I was crass. I lost control."

"Did you never lose control with Sarah?"

"Not on our wedding night."

"Well firstly, this is not our wedding night and secondly, that is much to Sarah's detriment because you look magnificent when you lose control."

"You do not have to be polite, Harriet."

Harriet lifted her hand to her mouth and laughed.

Then she raised her other hand running it through his damp hair, caring naught that she splashed herself with his perspiration.

"Oh Stephen, I am polite when I am in a duchess's drawing room for afternoon tea or a countess's ballroom or being introduced to a viscountess in Hyde Park during the fashionable hour. I believe that with you atop me, my shift and your shirt all a-tangle, my body tingling from your ministrations and after a day of chasing after my brother and his pregnant ex-kitchen maid fiancée up the Great North Road, politeness is not high up on my list of priorities. Since the moment you first kissed me, I have loved every second of what we have done. I look forward to our wedding night when I become your wife in every sense of the word. But I shall not force the issue now until the wedding is over."

He stared at her for a long moment then bent his head and kissed her softly.

"Thank you," he said quietly before moving off her and to the side, tugging her against him as he went. He adjusted his shirt, wiping his stomach with the fabric, then he adjusted her shift.

"Now can I touch it?" She giggled.

"No," he murmured, giving her an admonishing tap on the bottom. She giggled into his chest. "It is time for sleep."

"I suppose it is. But Stephen, thank you for tonight. I really have enjoyed it."

"So have I, my love. More than you could ever know."

"Mmm!" She snuggled against him, one hand nestled between their bodies, the other lying over his hip. It was not long before she could feel moments of consciousness being snatched away by slumber. She burrowed her face into the crook of his arm and he murmured contentedly, throwing his free arm around her.

Marrying Stephen may yet be the best decision she had ever made.

****

Stephen was aware of the warm body at his side as consciousness filtered into his strange dream. The warm body was beginning to stir and the small hand on his chest was moving south.

"That hand had better not move any lower, Lady Harriet, or I shall not be responsible for my actions."

"And who said I wanted you to be responsible?"

He caught her hand and moved half over her, lifting her hand above her head, grinding his morning hardness into her thigh.

"Much though I would love to, it is not quite dawn. I believe if we make a move quickly, there is a good chance we shall catch up to your brother. I doubt he shall be on his way early. He is not much of a morning person and I do not want to spend more time than necessary chasing him up the Great North Road. So rather than pre-empting our vows, might I suggest we dress quickly and start travelling. I already asked for a breakfast to be packed into your picnic hamper."

"I see. That was very sensible of you."

"Do not think for one moment it is because I do not want to spend today in this bed making love to you, Harriet."

"Thank you for caring for William and doing your best to ensure his safety. I could not ask for more. I would rather we found William than stay here. There will be time enough for this." She waved her hand around to show she meant marital relations in general. He pressed a quick kiss to her lips before he reluctantly rolled off her and climbed out of bed, hastily finding his breeches. He forced himself not to look around at Harriet, and was aware when she scurried into the dressing room, having grabbed her valise and a few other necessities. He hoped he had done the right thing.

He had to admit to himself that physically and mentally he felt better after last night's events. He now felt that come the wedding night he would be able to make a better account of himself and ensure Harriet's pleasure before finding his own release.

It did not take long for them to be ready and the servants had the carriage prepared and picnic hamper stowed under the seat. Harriet looked bright and well-groomed despite not having a maid to help her dress. Stephen felt slightly tired but happy despite his concern for William.

How had they fared last night?

Harriet smiled as she accepted his hand to be helped into the carriage and they were off quickly, pulling back out onto the Great North Road, ready to stop at every inn on the way, praying that nothing had untoward had happened to William and Mary.

"Would you like something to eat?" he asked Harriet as she adjusted herself against the squabs half an hour after they had set off.

"No, thank you. I am not hungry."

"My love, you must eat."

Harriet turned and looked at him.

"Stephen, my brother is still missing, it is very early and we are in a moving carriage. I did not sleep particularly well. At present I do not want to eat anything. Please do not treat me as if I am made of porcelain or as if I am incapable of deciding whether I should eat or not."

"I am not suggesting you are incapable." He pulled off his top hat and ran his fingers through his hair, mussing it slightly. "I am just trying to care for you. I did a poor job of it last night. I should never have... well... found my pleasure the way I did."

"I do not recall any complaints from me, my lord. Believe me, if I had been disgruntled, I would have been the first to protest your treatment of me." He stared at her for a moment—still quite unable to believe how he had managed to become engaged to such a wonderful and clever woman. "You know I want more, Stephen. You know I want to become a real woman. You know my innocence is yours for the taking."

"I do—and I shall take it—on our wedding night."

"I do not know if I can wait that long after last night. What was rubbing against me through our clothes is nothing like the paintings in the art galleries. I must say that you have piqued my curiosity."

He laughed out loud. Then he leaned and pressed a soft kiss to her lips. Long enough for her to know how very much he wanted her and how much he regretted that he could not lay her down on the seat of the carriage and have her here and now, but short enough that he did not lose his sanity. "Believe me when I say that your discomfiture over the wait shall be nothing compared to mine."

"I beg to differ. You have at least experienced the delights of the marriage bed. However, now is not the time to discuss it. It appears we have arrived at the next inn."

He peered out the window and realised that the coach was indeed slowing and turning into a courtyard. The inn was in reasonable condition and a good size. Had they carried on last night to this inn, they would possibly have found two rooms available and they would not have had a wonderful night of pleasure and frustration. He would not have known the sounds Harriet made as he sucked on her nipples or moved his middle finger through her cleft, circling the little nub that made her wriggle and groan. He shook his head and tugged at his waistcoat, hoping the signs that he was beginning to become aroused were not obvious.

"You look lost in thought," said Harriet, breaking into his cerebral meanderings. "About what were you thinking?"

He turned to her and grinned. "You," he said without preamble. "And last night."

Colour flooded her cheeks and neck, her eyes widened and her pink lips made a perfect 'o.'

"You said that just to discompose me, you vexing man," she hissed as he stepped out of the carriage.

"I said it because it was the truth. However the thought of you last night had me rather discomposed. Why should I be the only one in this relationship who is discomposed?"

She narrowed her eyes as he helped her down from the carriage. Then she looked around the courtyard, her gaze settling on a coach which was being readied. The team of four were not the best horses in the world but they were good enough cattle.

"Do you think that might be William's hired carriage? It does look rather like the sort of carriage that is hired. It has no livery or coat of arms."

When she turned to him her eyes shone bright.

"Do not get your hopes up, my love. There are hired carriages all the way up and down the Great North Road. Most people do not own their own carriages. Most cannot afford it. You are in a very privileged position because you were the daughter, and now are the sister, of an earl."

"I suppose you are correct. It would be too much to hope for that we would find them here."

They crossed the courtyard and into the inn where they found a small desk and a large man standing behind it writing in some kind of ledger. He had huge hairy sideburns, grey hair and twinkling blue eyes.

"Good morning my lord, my lady." He looked a little askance. It must not be common for people to turn up at breakfast time.

Before Stephen could open his mouth, Harriet spoke. Throughout their journey yesterday, Stephen had been the one to jump out of the carriage at all the inns and ask about the missing couple. He didn't really know why he had helped Harriet down from the carriage when they had arrived here, except for the fact he had been distracted.

"We are sorry to bother you, but my brother and his lady are travelling up the Great North Road to Scotland, we believe. We are concerned about them. You see, my brother is… well he has difficulties with understanding, as does his young lady. We are not trying to stop them. I am happy for them to marry. But they do not know how very far away Scotland is and I fear they may be set upon by highwaymen or unscrupulous people who may take advantage. He is my only family and I would be devastated if something were to happen to him. He may use his title, Lord Oldbeck, or his family name Weatherby. Oh please…" Harriet's voice broke and she reached for a handkerchief. "Perhaps they stopped in here yesterday or maybe even stayed the night. Any news would be of the utmost help."

"They are here, my lady," said the innkeeper hastily, raising his hands as if hoping to staunch the flow of tears. "Please do not distress yourself. They have my best suite of rooms. Two rooms with a dressing room adjoining. I am so very sorry. They said they were wed. I didn't know."

She waved away the apology and sniffled into her handkerchief.

"Would you mind showing us to their room?"

"Right away."

The man led the way and Stephen followed behind. He had never seen Harriet so distressed before. As they reached the stairs he placed a hand on her back.

"We shall stay here a while and allow you to rest, my love. You are quite overset," he whispered to her when he thought they might be out of earshot. She turned to him, holding the handkerchief in such a way that it would hide her face from the innkeeper and rolled her dry eyes at him, giving him an incredulous look. The minx was acting. Why had he not realised? Now he felt like the imbecile. She sniffed loudly for good measure as they reached the top of the stairs.

When they reached the door the innkeeper indicated,

Stephen thanked him, assured him he would be compensated and dismissed him, and then took over.

"Oldbeck, open the door."

"Charville, is that you?" came William's voice from inside—a mixture of fear and relief.

"Aye. Now you're not in trouble but you need to let Harriet and me in."

"Harriet is here?"

"Yes. Now open the door."

It took about a minute before the scrape of metal on wood indicated William had obeyed the instruction. William stood, head bowed, eyes downcast towards his stockinged feet, his hair unkempt. Inside the room Mary stood dressed in a manner of speaking though her dress gaped, suggesting her stays were not tightly tied. Her cheeks were tear-stained.

"Mary?" said Harriet, hurrying over to her charge and putting her arm around the young woman. "What is the matter?"

"I... I... couldn't tie William's cravat."

Harriet looked over at Stephen and as their gazes met, he read relief in her eyes.

"Oh Mary, that's why William has a valet. I doubt I could tie Stephen's cravat either."

Stephen looked at the offending garment hanging off William's neck and set about fixing it.

"She didn't wind it around your neck enough times, old boy," he muttered. "Now hold still and behave or I'll be tempted to throttle you with the damned thing for all the trouble you've caused."

"I thought you would be pleased. You said you would be glad when we wed."

"Yes, I did, but I did not mean for you to hare off to Scotland. Do you have any idea the distance between Scotland and London?"

"Not really but I think it's quite far away. But people go to Scotland to get wed all the time."

"Only in books, my man, only in books. It takes five to seven days, depending on the state of the roads. More sometimes."

"Really?"

"Yes. So ask before you carry out another one of your schemes. You know I am here to help you, else why would Harriet put herself through marrying a grumpy old second son of a duke like me?"

William patted Stephen on the shoulder as he finished straightening the simple knot.

"Because she loves you. Anyone can see that. Even I can see that, Charville." Then he let out an overly-loud guffaw. "You did not know?"

"I think you are wrong, Oldbeck."

"You are the one who is wrong and I promise you, Charville, if you hurt Harry, I will kill you. You had better love her back."

"You cannot force a man to love someone."

"I bloody well can." Oldbeck's voice had started to rise and there was fire in his eyes. Stephen held up his hand and stayed the fellow's ire.

"But in this instance there is no need. I believe I may already be falling in love with her."

"You had better be."

"All right, old fellow. No need to threaten me. Now I propose that we get these young ladies down the nearest altar, get them married to us before they change their minds and travel back to London as quickly as horses can transport us."

"Marry Mary today? But we are not in Scotland."

"No, but you have your licence, do you not?"

"I do."

"Then we can marry. I have mine too."

"Oh."

"Yes. And for the record, you did not need the licence for Scotland. They have different laws up there."

"Yes, my driver told me."

"Shame he did not tell you how far away Scotland is. Now, shall we go and see about our transportation back to London and find out where is the nearest church?"

"Good idea," said Oldbeck, clapping Stephen on the shoulder before shrugging on his tight-fitting coat and following him out the room and down the narrow staircase.

"That is the coach driver. I paid him all the money to Scotland," said Oldbeck when they came out into the sunlit courtyard.

"How much money?"

"I cannot remember. He told me and it seemed a lot but I do not know how much a trip to Scotland costs."

Stephen strode over to the man. He was well-dressed for a man who drove a carriage for a living. Did he usually take advantage of the less fortunate? He approached quietly. The man was checking over one of the horses at the front of his team.

"If I find out that you have overcharged the gentleman you are driving to Scotland," Stephen muttered in a menacing tone in the man's ear, "then so help me God but I shall tear you limb from limb before I have you in front of a magistrate for theft."

The driver turned slowly, pushing himself against the horse. He was about half a head shorter than Stephen but he did not flinch. He look Stephen in the eye, scowling.

"Mr Weatherby has been charged a fair price for the journey. I took the money up front because he seemed unsure as to how far away Scotland was and I did not believe he had enough money to pay me. I didn't want to arrive in Scotland to find myself without any wages for a job well done. Here's the money he gave me." The man pulled a small leather pouch out of his pocket and handed it to Stephen. Stephen opened it and looked at the coins. It seemed a fair amount of money to him for a journey that might last a week.

"And how do I know this is all he gave you?"

"Ask him." The driver nodded to Oldbeck who was standing behind him, his eyes like saucers.

Oldbeck shuffled over and looked in the pouch.

"Yes, that is right."

"Earlier you said you could not remember."

"I couldn't remember the number but I can remember the coins. There were five of those, and eight of those and three of those."

"I see."

"Charville, he gave me good advice last night too. Told me to say I was married to Mary so that I could keep her safe. And to organise a private parlour in which to eat."

"It seems you shall be driving us back to London Mr…"

"Graves."

"Mr Graves. If you do not mind. Please accept my apologies. I am a little overprotective of my brother-in-law-to-be. Please keep the money as your wages for the inconvenience. And now we must find a church to marry both of our beautiful brides."

Chapter Fourteen

Harriet moved to the seat beside the hearth and picked up the glass of wine which she had poured. She had asked for the bottle and goblets to be brought to her room rather than tea. She felt she needed something to help steady her after the events of the day.

First they had come across William and Mary in an inn before Stephen had whisked them all off for an intimate double wedding ceremony at a small village church. William had looked delighted and Mary had beamed. Her skin was beginning to glow and Harriet could not help thinking that they were going to have to start letting out her dresses at the bodice. Her breasts were practically overflowing, something that the poor vicar seemed to have noticed and had made a conscious effort not to allow his gaze to wander towards.

The journey had seemed interminable after that. Stephen had seemed gruff, giving monosyllabic answers and staring morosely out of the carriage windows. When at last she had lost her temper with him in a most unladylike fashion, he had admitted it was because he desired her and was finding the enclosed carriage rather unbearable. She had suggested he ride the rest of the way on horseback but he had refused, saying it was unconscionable to leave her alone on her wedding day and he could survive it. He had given her a wan smile then leaned over and pressed a delicate kiss on her lips, before retreating back into his corner to scowl ferociously.

Now William and Mary were in the Oldbeck townhouse, consummating their marriage, Harriet supposed, and she was waiting for her new husband to come to her. She was wearing the transparent nightrail that Lizzie had helped her purchase and a silk dressing gown over the top.

She started when there was a light tap at the door connecting her room to the dressing room between their bedchambers.

The door opened and Stephen stood there biting into his lower lip—the first time she had ever seen any real sign of hesitation from him. His hair was damp from his bath, curling at the collar of his dark blue silk dressing gown. He held a glass of whisky in his hand.

He lifted his glass to her and she lifted hers in a silent toast. His lips broke into a sunny smile and he stepped further into the room, closing the door with a click.

She stood as he approached.

"Good evening… husband."

"Ah… that sounds almost erotic when you say it like that." He lifted his hand and touched his thumb to the centre of her lips, trailing it gently to the side. She darted out her tongue and licked it.

Stephen arched an eyebrow and she moved her head slightly, enough to capture his thumb and suck it into her mouth.

His eyes seemed to darken instantly, his knuckles of the other hand whitening as he grasped the glass more tightly.

"Bloody hell, Harriet, there is nothing innocent about you, my love."

She pulled back, blindly reaching for the table to lay her glass down.

"I… of course I am. Steph…"

"Oh God no!" He had enveloped her in his embrace before she had a chance to step back, his whisky sloshing down the back of her dressing gown. "I did not mean to suggest that you are not a virgin. Christ, no. I meant… how do I put it? You see some women have an innate sensuality about them. When you took my thumb into your mouth, you were acting on instinct. It shows you have that innate sensuality. That was what I meant. I was not casting aspersions or suggesting you are not innocent in the sense of still being a virgin. Please, Harriet, it was clumsy of me to say it. It was really meant to be a compliment. I am just so out of practice that I continually say the wrong things. As I already told you, it has been a long time since I made love to a woman."

She breathed in and pushed her arms around him, laying her head on his chest.

"Oh Stephen, was last night not making love?"

"It was… in a manner of speaking."

"Well then, it has only been one day since you made love to a woman. And she enjoyed it very much. Now would you put down that whisky before it drips down my back in its entirety?"

"Oh yes."

He placed the whisky next to her wine then led her over to the bed. Then Stephen untied her robe and pushed it off her shoulders. He made a low whistling noise.

"Lizzie helped you make an exquisite choice, my lady."

"I am glad you approve."

He chuckled.

"You could wear a coal sack and I would approve. You would look beautiful in anything. But let me remove this. I am not sure I trust myself not to rip it tonight." She lifted her arms and tugged it at her waist, revealing her calves, her knees, her thighs. She bit her lip as the hem skimmed her hips. Oh he could see right through it. He could see the triangle of hair covering her feminine parts and her nipples and the shape of her breasts. But the removal of this last barrier made it final.

Stephen adjusted his grip and Harriet lifted her arms. He pulled the garment over her torso and head, her loose braid slapping against her back again as he threw the fabric onto the floor.

"Now you," she said breathlessly, fighting the urge to cover herself with her arms. He stood, his gaze fixed on her breasts, as if mesmerised by a fae from the stories she used to read as a child.

Harriet undid the knot of his dressing gown, letting the ties fall, then she placed the palms of her hand on his chest, pressing them up towards his shoulders, watching the slippery fabric slide off his muscles, revealing curly dark hair across his chest, not too thick but enough to look masculine and virile and to send Harriet's pulse racing. She had been vaguely aware of it last night when the neck of his shirt was open but now she ran the tips of three fingers through it. It was softer than it looked.

Something touched her belly, like the wet nose of a dog. She looked down at his male member, hard and straight, it jerked slightly. She was almost sure the thing was looking at her out of the slit on the end. And it seemed terribly big. She gulped down a gasp of surprise. Surely that would not fit inside her.

"Harriet?"

"Will it hurt terribly much?" she asked—embarrassed that her confidence had deserted her at this crucial moment.

"I...I do not know, if I am truly honest with you, my love. But Sarah seemed no worse the wear after our wedding night and I know of no other women who seems to have been traumatised by losing their virginity. Lizzie seems fine. I really think the best thing to do is to get it over with. I shall do my best to be gentle. I promise you that."

She nodded, her gaze having never left his hard length.

"Thank you," she replied, annoyed at the tremble in her voice. Stephen let out a frustrated little snort and pulled down the bedcovers.

"Harriet, love, it is not a lot different to last night."

"I know. But my maidenhead. It is just… Oh, is there no other way to breach it and just get it over with?"

He chuckled, indicating she should climb into bed. She did.

"You make it sound as if making love to your husband is a chore."

"I am sorry."

He climbed in beside her. "I hate peas, you know."

"What?" Why the hell was he talking about peas at a time like this?

"Cannot stand the things. I do believe they may be the worst vegetable in the world."

"Not cabbage?"

"No, I do not mind cabbage. Why? Do you dislike cabbage?"

"No." Why was she lying in the nude with a naked man half on top of her discussing the vegetables they preferred, even if the naked man was her husband? She glanced down again at his member. It still looked slightly threatening to her. She wanted to touch it though. Was it as hard as it looked?

"The point about the peas is that, as a boy, I used to eat all my peas first, then I could savour the rest of my food, having got the nasty bit out of the way."

Was Stephen Charville going with this conversation where she thought he was going?

"My Lord, in this little parable, is my maidenhead…"

"The peas. Yes." He sounded triumphant as he gathered her in his arms and pressed his lips to hers. Part of her felt she should be insulted but when he used his tongue to part her lips, she melted into him, trying to memorise the sensations of his body against hers. The hard planes of his muscles against her feminine curves. His hard length digging into her thigh. His fingers digging into her thigh as he bent her knee and pressed it onto the mattress, opening her up to him. He skimmed his fingers up the inside of her thigh as he kissed down her neck. Her head was pressed back against the pillow.

His featherlike kisses were driving her wild. Then his fingers touched her on her delicate inner folds. The lightest touch. A tickling sensation that made her moan. He moved his finger so slowly that she felt she might die of longing. The he dipped one finger to her entrance without breaching.

"You are wet already, my love. Were you anticipating my arrival?"

More kisses down her chest.

"Of course," she managed. Why was he so slow? Last night he had all but ravished her breasts by now.

"And what did you anticipate me doing to you?"

She swallowed. What could he mean?

"I... making me your wife."

He brought his mouth closer to her nipple. She squirmed, hoping he would understand what she wanted.

"But where did you imagine me kissing you, suckling you, nipping you, caressing you, touching you?

Ah, she understood.

"My breasts... on my nipples. Oh please, Stephen. I need you." She arched her back. But before he took her nipple in his mouth he lifted his hand sucked his finger, wetting it thoroughly. Then he closed his lips over the distended peak and she forgot everything.

Until he pressed the finger inside her. It was not unpleasant and within a few moments it became pleasurable. She began to move against the finger. He lifted his head from her breast, removed his finger and sucked a second digit. This time she was prepared for the intrusion. She suspected she tensed slightly and he cooed against her flesh, kissing around her areola and using his thumb to make circles around another part of her feminine flesh. But those circles were anything but soothing. She was beginning to rock against his movements.

"You are ready." He lifted himself into the cradle of her thighs and looked deep into her eyes. His smile was encouraging. "Your body is made to do this, my love. Countless women have done it before you and will do it after you. There is nothing to fear."

She nodded. She knew she was being silly.

He moved his hard flesh through her folds as he bent his head and kissed her thoroughly. This was like last night, but without the clothing between them. The moisture from her own flesh allowed him to glide easily, to ramp up her need for him. She speared her fingers through his hair and angled his head, taking control of the kiss for the first time.

Stephen moved his hand and began to fumble between them. This was it. Harriet shut her eyes, concentrated on the kiss, but Stephen had to break away to position himself at her entrance. She willed herself not to tense, not to cry out if it was painful. She wanted to make this pleasurable for him too.

He pressed into her and she stretched to accommodate him. There was no pain—not yet. He was watching her.

"Put your legs behind my back," he said. She did as he asked, then he placed his mouth on her shoulder. "I'm sorry," he muttered. He pushed into her in one determined movement. A sharp pain in that region as if she had been stabbed was gone before she had time to truly acknowledge it.

He withdrew and pushed in again. It was slightly uncomfortable this time but not painful.

He withdrew again and this time he rolled off her and onto his back.

"Come sit astride me." She looked at him in consternation. Astride him? Like a man sits a horse? "One leg on one side of my hips, the other on this side." He tapped alternate sides of the sheet. She followed his instructions, placing her hands on his shoulders to get her balance, not placing her weight on him and eyeing his manhood that jerked against his stomach, now glistening with her slick juices and streaked slightly with blood. He

Lady Harriet's Unusual Reward

took himself in hand and moved the head until it was at her opening. "Sit down on it—slowly—that's it."

It was exquisite. She watched his gaze. His eyes darkened. One hand moved to her hip to help guide her, the other held himself in place. And then he removed that hand, placing it on her other hip, pushing her down onto him. The flesh between her thighs met his warm skin. She was fully seated atop him. She gave him a small smile of triumph.

She glanced down to where they joined, her red hair mingled with his dark hair, his thumb lightly brushing against her thigh.

"Was it terribly sore?"

"It was sore for just a moment and then it was gone."

"Well, my love, you are fully breached. I can go no deeper. The peas, as it were, have been consumed. Now for the rest of the main course. And if you are very good, perhaps, dessert."

"That sounds wonderful. Stephen, is this normal?"

"Normal?"

"For the woman to be in this position?"

He cocked his head to the side and ran his hand up to her breast, gently tweaking her nipple.

"It is not abnormal. Perhaps unusual for a lady's first time." He pulled himself into a sitting position. She could feel him shift inside her and she squirmed. He lifted her breast to his lips, licking round the hard nub three times before sucking it into his mouth.

She gasped as he moved his arms around her, tugging at the ribbon that held her braid in place. Then he was combing his fingers through the braid, undoing it. She dropped her head back, enjoying the feel of the thick tresses tickling the skin on her back. She could not help herself. She began to move up and down his thick shaft.

"Mmm, yes, that's right, my love. Ride my cock."

She paused momentarily, shocked by his language. He had been about to latch onto her other breast but he raised his head, licking his lips.

"Ah yes, I do sometimes use vulgar language when I make love. Should have apologised in advance. Sorry."

Harriet giggled.

She moved slowly on him and he groaned, moving his mouth back towards her breast.

"So, if I'm riding your cock," she whispered. He laid his forehead on her collarbone and she was sure he uttered an oath. "What do you call my breasts?"

"Pardon?"

He looked up at her as if he was a schoolboy sitting a particularly difficult Latin test.

"What vulgar word do you use for breasts, Stephen?"

He waved a hand then seemed to give in.

"Tits," he spat out.

She grinned at him.

"Earlier, I told you I was anticipating you coming to me and you asked what I anticipated you doing to me. I anticipated you sucking on my tits." She pressed a kiss to his lips then pulled away to ride his cock as he'd requested. "Suck my tits, Stephen, please."

"Christ," he muttered as he took one in his mouth and placed his hands on her bottom, helping her to maintain a rhythm.

Harriet had no idea what she was doing. She was following her instincts, but it appeared to be working. She worked herself up and down his "cock," the front of her sex rubbing deliciously against his body, building the tension in her that had built last night. The one that had eventually seemed to explode and bring her such a wonderful release.

She tugged on his hair and he released her breast. She covered his mouth with hers and he entwined his fingers in her long curls. His tongue appeared to work in harmony with his cock, to the same beat, like a symphony of their bodies. She was so close. She drew her mouth away, resting her forehead on his, slowing her movements to get just the right angle to bring herself to the peak she had found the previous night.

"That's it, my darling. Find your release on my cock."

"Oh Stephen, I…"

"Shh, I know, my love."

"Oh God."

He pressed a thumb to her nipple and tugged. One, two three more thrusts and she found bliss. She gasped as her fingernails dug into the flesh of his shoulders. As she plunged once more onto his hard length—onto his cock, she buried her face into his neck, shuddering her release. He held her, rubbing her back for a few moments, before gathering her in his arms, turning them both and laying her on the mattress. She muttered her displeasure when he slipped out from her. He chuckled.

"It's seldom possible to turn and stay inside, though it can be done. Are you able to continue? You're not in pain, are you?"

"No, I can continue." She was a little tender but she wanted to see and feel his release inside her. She wanted him to lose control as she had done. He did not need further reassurance. He pressed his lips to hers and began to move in her deep and fast.

Harriet wrapped her legs around her hips and when he lifted her bottom to angle her hips, she felt him sink deeper. He was so very masculine as he moved inside her, searching for his own completion. His back muscles flexed under the tips of her fingers. She did not expect what happened next. Her sensitive flesh began to tingle again and instinctively she knew she was rising to another peak. She moved under him, ripping her mouth away from his.

"Oh Stephen, it's happening again," she gasped, half frightened, half in awe.

"Jesus, you're going to kill me, Harriet," he muttered into her skin, as he shifted his position and drove deeper into her. She moved with him and at last she understood that passage in the Bible about a man leaving his parents and becoming one flesh with his wife. This was what it meant. They were one being now. Working in complete harmony—towards the same end.

And they worked together for long minutes, pushing each other, helping each other, ramping up the desire and need in each other. But there was something almost leisurely in it when he abandoned her neck and sucked the aching peak of her breast into her mouth.

She was still near the edge of release but it remained just out of reach. And somehow she did not mind. Being joined to Stephen was what mattered.

Then he looked up from her breast and moved his head, kissing her lightly on the nose.

"We could do this all night, holding off our releases, but I fear it would make you unbearably sore in the morning."

"I am not in pain yet."

"I know, but I would feel like a cad if you were unable to walk tomorrow. Besides. It's time for dessert."

He withdrew from her then and planted kisses down her chest and then her belly. She watched in dawning horror as his lips moved nearer to the small thatch of red hair at the top of her thighs.

"Stephen!" she squealed, trying to bat him away. He laughed and caught her wrists.

"Trust me, love. You will like this."

"But you cannot mean to kiss me... *there.*"

"I mean to do more than kiss you."

"Stephen, you cannot," she all but wailed.

"Husband's prerogative, but... you must allow me to do it for three minutes and if you really do not like it, I shall stop after three minutes. You only have to say. But just like peas, you have to at least try it. That is fair, is it not?"

She could not really argue with that, no matter how embarrassing it may be. And he had not moments before had his cock inside there, so it was rather late to be missish about the whole thing. And now she was even using the word cock in her head. Oh dear, she would never again be able to chastise William for talk of tupping Mary.

Then he touched his tongue to her folds. One swipe and she forgot every concern she'd had.

"Oh, that is…" She had no adequate words.

He chuckled and adjusted her legs, settling in to his task. Harriet had never imagined anything could be so mind-alteringly exquisite and decadent. Now she understood what the word erotic actually meant. His tongue swept along her cleft before he sucked the swollen flesh near her hairline into his mouth, sending her nearly into an abyss of sexual pleasure. She writhed under him, one hand scrunching his hair, attempting to direct him, while the other held tightly to the cotton sheet and she fought for some kind of purchase—some way to remain in reality as Stephen attempted to send her into sweet insanity.

Suddenly he rose up and entered her again, apologising, driving into her as he gathered her into his arms. She wrapped herself around him tightly. It only took a couple of thrusts before her body clamped around him.

"Bloody hell," he muttered into her hair. "I'm going to come." His movements were jerking and lacking in any sort of rhythm, but he continued to plunge into her. "I love you," he ground out, as he strained into her, his body hard and tense. The warmth of his seed filled Harriet, washing her insides and soothing her flesh that only now she realised probably did hurt a little. But her own body was still fluttering around his cock in the aftermath of her release and she was still slightly reeling from the words he had grunted when he had released his seed.

Lord Stephen Charville loved her. Oh she knew he held her in some kind of affection and they got on well. But love had not been something she had expected. Though she knew that somewhere along the line, she had fallen in love with him. She had just been unwilling to admit it. Not even to herself.

His breathing was beginning to slow and she could not help thinking that Stephen was trying to work out what to say next.

"Would it help if I said I love you too," she said, running a finger slowly down his damp spine.

"Only if it's true," he said onto her hair and the mattress.

"I love you too and that's the truth."

"Even when I compare your maidenhead to peas?"

"Even then."

He lifted himself, withdrawing from her, both of them wincing slightly.

"Lie on the pillows," he urged. Then he climbed off the bed and walked towards the dressing table. Her heart plunged. He was leaving her already. She had hoped… Well she was not entirely sure what she had hoped for. Her parents had kept separate bedchambers so she knew he would go back to his room.

Instead he poured some water from her pitcher into the bowl then lifted a linen, dipped it in water then wrung it out. He approached the bed again, a dry linen in his other hand.

"Let me wash between your legs. You shall be more comfortable." She opened her thighs and he wiped gently, then dried, before swiping both cloths over his now limp member. She was surprised at how much smaller it looked. He took them back over to the basin and left them by the side. Then he returned to the bed, pulling the covers over both of them as he climbed in beside her.

She laid her head on his shoulder and he placed a hand on her hip, encouraging her to lay her leg over both of his.

"This is nice."

"Harriet, would you mind sharing a bed? I could move to my own bed when you have your courses or if you are unwell or when you are with child and uncomfortable and when you are nursing our child but at other times, would you be averse to sharing a bed with me?"

She looked up into his dark eyes. He ran his hand through his hair, then tucked a red curl behind her ear.

"No, not at all. I… think I would prefer it. Did you share a bed with Sarah?"

"Sometimes but not as often as I would have liked. She came from a rather strict and old-fashioned family and I think her mother had put notions in her head about sharing a bed with her husband."

"Will the servants talk?"

"Servants do as their masters and mistresses tell them to do. Good servants say nothing outside the house. But it is not unusual for a husband and wife to share a bed. I did notice there was enough blood on the sheet that the maids will not gossip in the morning."

"The maids would gossip?"

"Oh I have no doubt. Had there been none, they would have assumed you were not innocent."

"That is terrible. What business is it of theirs?"

"None, but they would have gossiped anyway. In the same way that people will gossip when your new sister-in-law delivers a perfectly healthy baby in seven months."

"Ah, yes."

"Indeed. But no matter. We shall be in the country and by the time we come back to town, there shall be a new scandal to take away everyone's interest from the new Countess of Oldbeck.

"When should we return to the country?"

"A few days? We shall have a ball to celebrate both sets of nuptials. And a family dinner. Phoebe shall be upset that she missed it, but we can perhaps take her for a picnic in Hyde Park to make up for it."

"Oh that would be lovely. I shall arrange for a new gown and new hair ribbons for her. That should cheer her up."

"We can give Miss Paton time to prepare to travel to her new home. Then I must buy another coach. We shall be a merry little party as we head back to Oldbeck estate."

"Do you think we shall be happy?"

He lifted his head and pressed a kiss to her nose. "You know, I believe we shall."

"What about William's babe?"

"I believe he or she shall be fine too."

"What if it is like its mother and father?"

"Then we shall cross that bridge when we arrive at it. But from what you say, whatever is wrong with William was complication from his birth. And as for Mary… well, I guess we shall never know. But William has managed and this child will have Phoebe and cousins around it to help it out. Let us not worry until we have to. I would wager that William does not have a care in the world tonight."

"No, he will not."

"Then, my beautiful love, snuggle into me and claim your reward."

"My reward?"

"Your reward for saving Phoebe's life."

"Oh yes. I owe you an apology it seems. You are a gentleman of honour, Lord Stephen Charville."

"Honour and good taste, Lady Stephen Charville."

Epilogue

Ten years later

"Mama, may Eleanor and I go riding?"

Harriet arrived at the bottom of the stairs and looked at Phoebe, all grown up and looking more like Stephen every day. She was going to break hearts when she was let loose on the marriage mart in a couple of years. She fidgeted with the ribbons of her riding bonnet and bounced on her toes. Harriet had always struggled to say no to her stepdaughter and even more so to her nine-year-old niece who looked expectantly at her.

"Please, Aunt Harriet. Papa said to ask you. He seems upset again."

"All right then, run along. But where are the others?"

"I think they are all in the nursery. No one else wanted to ride. They said they were going to ask you and Papa to take them swimming in the lake after lunch," said Phoebe over her shoulder as she headed for the grand entrance of the old manor.

"Are they indeed," she said to no one in particular.

"Harry," came William's voice. "Please, can I talk to you?"

Harriet ushered her brother into the drawing room and closed the door. He started to pace.

"William, what is the matter?"

He stopped pacing, looked as if he was about to speak,

then started pacing again.

"It's Ellie. She knows."

"Knows what?"

"That I'm an imbecile."

"William, please do not use that word."

"Why, Harry, it's true."

Harriet sighed. "What does she know? How does she know?"

"Some boys in the village called me it in her hearing and she was in the library and she found a note I had written to Mary. I had just told her I had gone to the stables and may be late for dinner. The day the horse was foaling. You know I cannot spell and my writing is a mess and she saw it and she asked me about it. I just shouted at her to get out and, oh God, Harry, what have I done? She was in Phoebe's room. She was crying her heart out."

"She will understand, William. Once you tell her the truth."

"The truth?"

"Yes, William, the truth."

"What do I say?"

"That you find words and writing very difficult. And that understanding can be difficult too. And that sometimes people call you unkind names because of it. But none of that makes you love her any less. Tell her you were afraid that the unkind words would make her love you less and that is why you shouted. But William, I do promise that she will not love you less. In all the years that you and I have been on this earth together, my love for you as a brother has but grown. And that child loves you. And so do your other two children. You will always be her Papa, no matter how bad your spelling is."

"Do you really believe that?"

"I do."

She drew William into a hug then released him.

"Go and tell Mary. Let her know what is to come. You both need to be prepared. You need to decide if you should mention that she has similar difficulties. But only you and she can decide that."

"Thank you, Harriet. You look like you need to see Charville. He's in the study."

"Thank you."

She picked up her skirts and hurried as fast as her feet would carry her to the man who had been at her side almost constantly since the day they had wed.

He was on his feet as soon as the door of the study clicked shut. Harriet rushed into his arms and he enveloped her in his arms. He was not wearing a jacket. She buried her nose in the silk of his waistcoat and snuggled into the warmth of his body. Once she had explained what had happened with William she was pleased that Stephen agreed that her course of action was right.

****

Later that evening, the children arrived downstairs for dinner, William looked much more at ease, but he gave Ellie a wary glance as she walked into the dining room. She gave him her usual sunny smile. It was custom in the Oldbeck manor for the children to join the adults once a week for dinner. Suddenly Ellie threw her arms around her father's neck.

"I love you, Papa."

Phoebe walked up to Harriet, whom she had called Mama since the day after Stephen and Harriet had married, and bent down to Harriet's ear.

"She has known he is an imbecile for about two years. She has seen his writing before and they say it all the time in the village. Some of the staff here sometimes say it too. She was only upset because he shouted at her. And before you say anything else, I would never normally use that word to describe my uncle. I only use it now to explain that Ellie already knows what people say."

Harriet turned to Phoebe, her mouth wide open. Phoebe shrugged and raised a placating hand.

"Why did you not say anything before?"

"I thought you knew."

"Clearly not."

"Did she know about Mary?"

"She was not so sure about her mother. Aunt Mary hides it better. But she knew her mother could not read and write."

"I see."

"But all's well that ends well. She loves her parents and they love her. And young Benjamin will make a wonderful earl when the time comes. Not that Uncle William is not a great earl in his own right, of course."

Harriet's gaze fell on five-year-old Benjamin who was making a horse fly through the air with whooshing sounds. There was no sign that any of William's three children had any difficulties in learning and for that she was grateful.

"My horse has an invisible knight who will slay St George's dragon," called out the young viscount. Harriet laughed. Then she caught her husband's gaze. Thanks to him, Oldbeck was safe to pass on to the next generation. And in the next ten years, they would have built their own house on a piece of land adjoining the Oldbeck estate. It would be passed down to Henry, their two-year-old son and generous dowries would be given to Sarah, and Caroline, their seven and five-year-old daughters.

As she looked around her happy, laughing family it seemed that Lady Harriet had got much more than the reward she had originally requested for saving Lord Stephen Charville's daughter on that fateful sunny day at Lady Hawthorne's house party.

THE END

About the Author

Em lives in a small village on the West coast of Scotland. She has lots of interests including the regency period, science fiction and politics—politics being the thing that seems to get her into most trouble. She loves attending conventions, knitting, reading, trying to decide whether vampires are real and visiting her three beautiful nieces.

Made in the USA
Charleston, SC
10 August 2015